WITHDRAWN

Other anthologies by Terry Carr:

THE BEST SCIENCE FICTION OF THE YEAR (TWO VOLUMES)
AN EXALTATION OF STARS
INTO THE UNKNOWN
NEW WORLDS OF FANTASY
NEW WORLDS OF FANTASY #2
NEW WORLDS OF FANTASY #3
ON OUR WAY TO THE FUTURE
THE OTHERS
SCIENCE FICTION FOR PEOPLE WHO HATE
  SCIENCE FICTION
THIS SIDE OF INFINITY
UNIVERSE 1
UNIVERSE 2

With Donald A. Wollheim:
WORLD'S BEST SCIENCE FICTION: 1965–1971
  (SEVEN VOLUMES)

UNIVERSE 3

RANDOM HOUSE 🏠 NEW YORK

Universe 3

EDITED BY

Terry Carr

CONTENTS

INTRODUCTION

The golden age of science fiction is now. When *aficionados* of this field get together, that's a standard topic of discussion: When was science fiction's golden age? Some people say the early forties, when John W. Campbell and a host of new writers like Heinlein, Sturgeon and van Vogt were transforming the entire field; others point to the early fifties, to H. L. Gold and Anthony Boucher and to such writers as Damon Knight, Alfred Bester and Ray Bradbury. Some will lay claims for the late sixties, when the new wave passed and names like Ballard, Disch and Aldiss came forward.

There are still people around, too, who'll tell you about 1929 and David H. Keller, E. E. Smith and Ray Cummings.

The clue in most cases is when the person talking first began to read science fiction. When it was all new, all of it was exciting. Years ago a friend of mine, Pete Graham, tersely answered the question "When was the golden age of science fiction?" by saying, "Twelve." He didn't have to explain further; we knew what he meant.

But it isn't totally a subjective matter; there are such things as real standards of quality, tricky as they may be to assess. You can tell a good writer when he brings to life a scene or an idea you've seen so often before that you thought it was used up. ("You can have him, all the thrill's gone out of him," said the man to Kenneth Patchen, handing him a dead mole.) You can recognize a good story when it makes you feel things you're not used to—even if they're old things: if it's been a while since you've felt them, old things get new again. And when enough good writers and good stories appear in the field, we have a "golden age."

All right, consider the science-fiction field today. When before have we had so many first-rate talents writing at once? Philip K. Dick, R. A. Lafferty, Poul Anderson, Ursula K. Le Guin, Samuel R. Delany, Alexei Panshin, Avram Davidson, Larry Niven, Clifford D. Simak, John Brunner, Robert Silverberg, Thomas M. Disch, Joanna Russ, Brian W. Aldiss, Roger Zelazny, D. G. Compton, Kurt Vonnegut . . . I'm sure you could name a dozen more. And there are remarkably good new writers coming into the field all the time.

If we had had these writers and their stories in 1950, or 1940, or 1929, we'd have considered them giants, and many of the works of those previous golden ages would have paled to insignificance by comparison.

But of course we couldn't have had all these writers then; science fiction evolves, it builds on the ideas and stories that have gone before. *The Three Stigmata of Palmer Eldritch* couldn't have been written in 1929; it would simply have been unthinkable. That's also true of *Stand on Zanzibar, And Chaos Died, Lord of Light, Slaughterhouse-Five, Camp Concentration* or *The Einstein Intersection*. Clifford Simak was active in science fiction in 1940, but he was writing *Cosmic Engineers*, not *Why Call Them Back From Heaven?*

Time offers progress, and new possibilities emerge. We live in an increasingly exciting world and amid larger realities than we dreamed of when science fiction was young. (If we date modern science fiction's birth from the founding of the first sf magazine, then science fiction was thirteen years old at the beginning of 1940.) The boundaries of scientific knowledge expand almost exponentially, and we're beginning to understand that there are other kinds of knowledge, too.

It's all here to be wondered at, and written about, and science fiction has developed the vocabulary for it. This is the literature of our infinite universe; is it any wonder that so many strongly talented writers should be drawn to it?

So the golden age is now. Part of it is here, in this book: enjoy, enjoy.

—TERRY CARR
Oakland, California
June 9, 1972

UNIVERSE 3

THE DEATH OF DOCTOR ISLAND

by Gene Wolfe

This fascinating novelette by Gene Wolfe is the story of a strange young boy who moved his head continually from side to side, as certain reptiles do, and of what happened between him and two others on a man-made satellite circling Jupiter. It may be the oddest sequel in science fiction: two years ago Wolfe wrote a short story titled "The Island of Dr. Death," which was nominated for a Nebula Award; Wolfe wondered what kind of story he might devise if he turned the themes and charactertypes upside down, and the result was the tale below. It's totally unconnected with the earlier story in any conventional sense; it's complete in itself and has no characters, background or situation from the

other story. It might be regarded as a fugue-sequel on earlier
themes . . . or you could ignore such quasi-technical jargon
and read the story purely for itself: a richly inventive tale of
people in an intriguing new environment.

I have desired to go
  Where springs not fail,
To fields where flies no sharp and sided hail
  And a few lilies blow.

And I have asked to be
  Where no storms come,
Where the green swell is in the havens dumb,
  And out of the swing of the sea.
                              —Gerard Manley Hopkins

A GRAIN of sand, teetering on the brink of the pit,
trembled and fell in; the ant lion at the bottom angrily flung
it out again. For a moment there was quiet. Then the entire
pit, and a square meter of sand around it, shifted drunkenly
while two coconut palms bent to watch. The sand rose, pivot-
ing at one edge, and the scarred head of a boy appeared—
a stubble of brown hair threatened to erase the marks of the
sutures; with dilated eyes hypnotically dark he paused, his
neck just where the ant lion's had been; then, as though
goaded from below, he vaulted up and onto the beach,
turned, and kicked sand into the dark hatchway from which
he had emerged. It slammed shut. The boy was about fourteen.

For a time he squatted, pushing the sand aside and trying
to find the door. A few centimeters down, his hands met a
gritty, solid material which, though neither concrete nor
sandstone, shared the qualities of both—a sand-filled organic

plastic. On it he scraped his fingers raw, but he could not locate the edges of the hatch.

Then he stood and looked about him, his head moving continually as the heads of certain reptiles do—back and forth, with no pauses at the terminations of the movements. He did this constantly, ceaselessly—always—and for that reason it will not often be described again, just as it will not be mentioned that he breathed. He did; and as he did, his head, like a rearing snake's, turned from side to side. The boy was thin, and naked as a frog.

Ahead of him the sand sloped gently down toward sapphire water; there were coconuts on the beach, and sea shells, and a scuttling crab that played with the finger-high edge of each dying wave. Behind him there were only palms and sand for a long distance, the palms growing ever closer together as they moved away from the water until the forest of their columniated trunks seemed architectural; like some palace maze becoming as it progressed more and more draped with creepers and lianas with green, scarlet and yellow leaves, the palms interspersed with bamboo and deciduous trees dotted with flaming orchids until almost at the limit of his sight the whole ended in a spangled wall whose predominant color was black-green.

The boy walked toward the beach, then down the beach until he stood in knee-deep water as warm as blood. He dipped his fingers and tasted it—it was fresh, with no hint of the disinfectants to which he was accustomed. He waded out again and sat on the sand about five meters up from the high-water mark, and after ten minutes, during which he heard no sound but the wind and the murmuring of the surf, he threw back his head and began to scream. His screaming was high-pitched, and each breath ended in a gibbering, ululant note, after which came the hollow, iron gasp of the next indrawn breath. On one occasion he had screamed in this way, without cessation, for fourteen hours and twenty-two minutes, at the end of which a nursing nun with an exemplary record stretching back seventeen years had administered an injection without the permission of the attending physician.

After a time the boy paused—not because he was tired, but in order to listen better. There was, still, only the sound of the wind in the palm fronds and the murmuring surf, yet he felt that he had heard a voice. The boy could be quiet as well as noisy, and he was quiet now, his left hand sifting white sand as clean as salt between its fingers while his right tossed tiny pebbles like beachglass beads into the surf.

"Hear me," said the surf. *"Hear me. Hear me."*

"I hear you," the boy said.

"Good," said the surf, and it faintly echoed itself: *"Good, good, good."*

The boy shrugged.

"What shall I call you?" asked the surf.

"My name is Nicholas Kenneth de Vore."

"Nick, *Nick . . . Nick?"*

The boy stood, and turning his back on the sea, walked inland. When he was out of sight of the water he found a coconut palm growing sloped and angled, leaning and weaving among its companions like the plume of an ascending jet blown by the wind. After feeling its rough exterior with both hands, the boy began to climb; he was inexpert and climbed slowly and a little clumsily, but his body was light and he was strong. In time he reached the top, and disturbed the little brown plush monkeys there, who fled chattering into other palms, leaving him to nestle alone among the stems of the fronds and the green coconuts. "I am here also," said a voice from the palm.

"Ah," said the boy, who was watching the tossing, sapphire sky far over his head.

"I will call you Nicholas."

The boy said, "I can see the sea."

"Do you know my name?"

The boy did not reply. Under him the long, long stem of the twisted palm swayed faintly.

"My friends all call me Dr. Island."

"I will not call you that," the boy said.

"You mean that you are not my friend."

A gull screamed.

"But you see, I take you for my friend. You may say that I am not yours, but I say that you are mine. I like you, Nicholas, and I will treat you as a friend."

"Are you a machine or a person or a committee?" the boy asked.

"I am all those things and more. I am the spirit of this island, the tutelary genius."

"Bullshit."

"Now that we have met, would you rather I leave you alone?"

Again the boy did not reply.

"You may wish to be alone with your thoughts. I would like to say that we have made much more progress today than I anticipated. I feel that we will get along together very well."

After fifteen minutes or more, the boy asked, "Where does the light come from?" There was no answer. The boy waited for a time, then climbed back down the trunk, dropping the last five meters and rolling as he hit in the soft sand.

He walked to the beach again and stood staring out at the water. Far off he could see it curving up and up, the distant combers breaking in white foam until the sea became white-flecked sky. To his left and his right the beach curved away, bending almost infinitesimally until it disappeared. He began to walk, then saw, almost at the point where perception was lost, a human figure. He broke into a run; a moment later, he halted and turned around. Far ahead another walker, almost invisible, strode the beach; Nicholas ignored him; he found a coconut and tried to open it, then threw it aside and walked on. From time to time fish jumped, and occasionally he saw a wheeling sea bird dive. The light grew dimmer. He was aware that he had not eaten for some time, but he was not in the strict sense hungry—or rather, he enjoyed his hunger now in the same way that he might, at another time, have gashed his arm to watch himself bleed. Once he said, "Dr. Island!" loudly as he passed a coconut palm, and then later began to chant "Dr. Island, Dr. Island, Dr. Island" as he walked until the words had lost all meaning. He swam in the sea as he had been taught to swim in the great quartanary treatment tanks on Callisto to improve his coordination, and spluttered and snorted until he learned to deal with the waves. When it was so dark he could see only the white sand and the white foam of the breakers, he drank from the sea and fell asleep on the beach, the right side of his taut, ugly face relaxing first, so that it seemed asleep even while the left eye was open and staring; his head rolling from side to side; the left corner of his mouth preserving, like a death mask, his characteristic expression—angry, remote, tinged with that inhuman quality which is found nowhere but in certain human faces.

When he woke it was not yet light, but the night was fading to a gentle gray. Headless, the palms stood like tall ghosts up and down the beach, their tops lost in fog and the lingering dark. He was cold. His hands rubbed his sides; he danced on the sand and sprinted down the edge of the lapping water in an effort to get warm; ahead of him a pinpoint of red light became a fire, and he slowed.

A man who looked about twenty-five crouched over the fire. Tangled black hair hung over this man's shoulders, and he had a sparse beard; otherwise he was as naked as Nicholas himself. His eyes were dark, and large and empty, like the ends of broken pipes; he poked at his fire, and the smell of roasting fish came with the smoke. For a time Nicholas stood at a distance, watching.

Saliva ran from a corner of the man's mouth, and he wiped it away with one hand, leaving a smear of ash on his face. Nicholas edged closer until he stood on the opposite side of the fire. The fish had been wrapped in broad leaves and mud, and lay in the center of the coals. "I'm Nicholas," Nicholas said. "Who are you?" The young man did not look at him, had never looked at him.

"Hey, I'd like a piece of your fish. Not much. All right?"

The young man raised his head, looking not at Nicholas but at some point far beyond him; he dropped his eyes again. Nicholas smiled. The smile emphasized the disjointed quality of his expression, his mouth's uneven curve.

"Just a little piece? Is it about done?" Nicholas crouched, imitating the young man, and as though this were a signal, the young man sprang for him across the fire. Nicholas jumped backward, but the jump was too late—the young man's body struck his and sent him sprawling on the sand; fingers clawed for his throat. Screaming, Nicholas rolled free, into the water; the young man splashed after him; Nicholas dove.

He swam underwater, his belly almost grazing the wave-rippled sand until he found deeper water; then he surfaced, gasping for breath, and saw the young man, who saw him as well. He dove again, this time surfacing far off, in deep water. Treading water, he could see the fire on the beach, and the young man when he returned to it, stamping out of the sea in the early light. Nicholas then swam until he was five hundred meters or more down the beach, then waded in to shore and began walking back toward the fire.

The young man saw him when he was still some distance off, but he continued to sit, eating pink-tinted tidbits from his fish, watching Nicholas. "What's the matter?" Nicholas said while he was still a safe distance away. "Are you mad at me?"

From the forest, birds warned, "Be careful, Nicholas."

"I won't hurt you," the young man said. He stood up,

wiping his oily hands on his chest, and gestured toward the fish at his feet. "You want some?"

Nicholas nodded, smiling his crippled smile.

"Come then."

Nicholas waited, hoping the young man would move away from the fish, but he did not; neither did he smile in return.

"Nicholas," the little waves at his feet whispered, "this is Ignacio."

"Listen," Nicholas said, "is it really all right for me to have some?"

Ignacio nodded, unsmiling.

Cautiously Nicholas came forward; as he was bending to pick up the fish, Ignacio's strong hands took him; he tried to wrench free but was thrown down, Ignacio on top of him. "Please!" he yelled. "Please!" Tears started into his eyes. He tried to yell again, but he had no breath; the tongue was being forced, thicker than his wrist, from his throat.

Then Ignacio let go and struck him in the face with his clenched fist. Nicholas had been slapped and pummeled before, had been beaten, had fought, sometimes savagely, with other boys; but he had never been struck by a man as men fight. Ignacio hit him again and his lips gushed blood.

He lay a long time on the sand beside the dying fire. Consciousness returned slowly; he blinked, drifted back into the dark, blinked again. His mouth was full of blood, and when at last he spit it out onto the sand, it seemed a soft flesh, dark and polymerized in strange shapes; his left cheek was hugely swollen, and he could scarcely see out of his left eye. After a time he crawled to the water; a long time after that, he left it and walked shakily back to the ashes of the fire. Ignacio was gone, and there was nothing left of the fish but bones.

"Ignacio is gone," Dr. Island said with lips of waves.

Nicholas sat on the sand, cross-legged.

"You handled him very well."

"You saw us fight?"

"I saw you; I see everything, Nicholas."

"This is the worst place," Nicholas said; he was talking to his lap.

"What do you mean by that?"

"I've been in bad places before—places where they hit you or squirted big hoses of ice water that knocked you down. But not where they would let someone else—"

"Another patient?" asked a wheeling gull.

"—do it."

"You were lucky, Nicholas. Ignacio is homicidal."

"You could have stopped him."

"No, I could not. All this world is my eye, Nicholas, my ear and my tongue; but I have no hands."

"I thought you did all this."

"Men did all this."

"I mean, I thought you kept it going."

"It keeps itself going, and you—all the people here—direct it."

Nicholas looked at the water. "What makes the waves?"

"The wind and the tide."

"Are we on Earth?"

"Would you feel more comfortable on Earth?"

"I've never been there; I'd like to know."

"I am more like Earth than Earth now is, Nicholas. If you were to take the best of all the best beaches of Earth, and clear them of all the poisons and all the dirt of the last three centuries, you would have me."

"But this isn't Earth?"

There was no answer. Nicholas walked around the ashes of the fire until he found Ignacio's footprints. He was no tracker, but the depressions in the soft beach sand required none; he followed them, his head swaying from side to side as he walked, like the sensor of a mine detector.

. . .

For several kilometers Ignacio's trail kept to the beach; then, abruptly, the footprints swerved, wandered among the coconut palms, and at last were lost on the firmer soil inland. Nicholas lifted his head and shouted, "Ignacio? Ignacio!" After a moment he heard a stick snap, and the sound of someone pushing aside leafy branches. He waited.

"Mum?"

A girl was coming toward him, stepping out of the thicker growth of the interior. She was pretty, though too thin, and appeared to be about nineteen; her hair was blond where it had been most exposed to sunlight, darker elsewhere. "You've scratched yourself," Nicholas said. "You're bleeding."

"I thought you were my mother," the girl said. She was a head taller than Nicholas. "Been fighting, haven't you. Have you come to get me?"

Nicholas had been in similar conversations before and normally would have preferred to ignore the remark, but he was lonely now. He said, "Do you want to go home?"

"Well, I think I should, you know."

"But do you want to?"

"My mum always says if you've got something on the stove you don't want to burn—she's quite a good cook. She really is. Do you like cabbage with bacon?"

"Have you got anything to eat?"

"Not now. I had a thing a while ago."

"What kind of thing?"

"A bird." The girl made a vague little gesture, not looking at Nicholas. "I'm a memory that has swallowed a bird."

"Do you want to walk down by the water?" They were moving in the direction of the beach already.

"I was just going to get a drink. You're a nice tot."

Nicholas did not like being called a "tot." He said, "I set fire to places."

"You won't set fire to this place; it's been nice the last couple of days, but when everyone is sad, it rains."

Nicholas was silent for a time. When they reached the sea, the girl dropped to her knees and bent forward to drink, her long hair falling over her face until the ends trailed in the water, her nipples, then half of each breast, in the water. "Not there," Nicholas said. "It's sandy, because it washes the beach so close. Come on out here." He waded out into the sea until the lapping waves nearly reached his armpits, then bent his head and drank.

"I never thought of that," the girl said. "Mum says I'm stupid. So does Dad. Do you think I'm stupid?"

Nicholas shook his head.

"What's your name?"

"Nicholas Kenneth de Vore. What's yours?"

"Diane. I'm going to call you Nicky. Do you mind?"

"I'll hurt you while you sleep," Nicholas said.

"You wouldn't."

Yes I would. At St. John's where I used to be, it was zero G most of the time, and a girl there called me something I didn't like, and I got loose one night and came into her cubical while she was asleep and nulled her restraints, and then she floated around until she banged into something, and that woke her up and she tried to grab, and then that made her bounce all around inside and she broke two fingers and her nose and got blood all over. The attendants came, and one told me—they didn't know then I did it—when he came out his white suit was, like, polka-dot red all over because wherever the blood drops had touched him they soaked right in."

The girl smiled at him, dimpling her thin face. "How did they find out it was you?"

"I told someone and he told them."

"I bet you told them yourself."

"I bet I didn't!" Angry, he waded away, but when he had stalked a short way up the beach he sat down on the sand, his back toward her.

"I didn't mean to make you mad, Mr. de Vore."

"I'm not mad!"

She was not sure for a moment what he meant. She sat down beside and a trifle behind him, and began idly piling sand in her lap.

Dr. Island said, "I see you've met."

Nicholas turned, looking for the voice. "I thought you saw everything."

"Only the important things, and I have been busy on another part of myself. I am happy to see that you two know one another; do you find you interact well?"

Neither of them answered.

"You should be interacting with Ignacio; he needs you."

"We can't find him," Nicholas said.

"Down the beach to your left until you see the big stone, then turn inland. About five hundred meters."

Nicholas stood up, and turning to his right, began to walk away. Diane followed him, trotting until she caught up.

"I don't like," Nicholas said, jerking a shoulder to indicate something behind him.

"Ignacio?"

"The doctor."

"Why do you move your head like that?"

"Didn't they tell you?"

"No one told me anything about you."

"They opened it up"—Nicholas touched his scars—"and took this knife and cut all the way through my corpus . . . corpus . . ."

"Corpus callosum," muttered a dry palm frond.

"—corpus callosum," finished Nicholas. "See, your brain is like a walnut inside. There are the two halves, and then right down in the middle a kind of thick connection of meat from one to the other. Well, they cut that."

"You're having a bit of fun with me, aren't you?"

"No, he isn't," a monkey who had come to the water line to look for shellfish told her. "His cerebrum has been surgically divided; it's in his file." It was a young monkey, with a trusting face full of small, ugly beauties.

Nicholas snapped, "It's in my head."

Diane said, "I'd think it would kill you, or make you an idiot or something."

"They say each half of me is about as smart as both of us were together. Anyway, this half is . . . the half . . . the *me* that talks."

"There are two of you now?"

"If you cut a worm in half and both parts are still alive, that's two, isn't it? What else would you call us? We can't ever come together again."

"But I'm talking to just one of you?"

"We both can hear you."

"Which one answers?"

Nicholas touched the right side of his chest with his right hand. "Me; I do. They told me it was the left side of my brain, that one has the speech centers, but it doesn't feel that way; the nerves cross over coming out, and it's just the right side of me, I talk. Both my ears hear for both of us, but out of each eye we only see half and half—I mean, I only see what's on the right of what I'm looking at, and the other side, I guess, only sees the left, so that's why I keep moving my head. I guess it's like being a little bit blind; you get used to it."

The girl was still thinking of his divided body. She said, "If you're only half, I don't see how you can walk."

"I can move the left side a little bit, and we're not mad at each other. We're not supposed to be able to come together at all, but we do: down through the legs and at the ends of the fingers and then back up. Only I can't talk with my other side because he can't, but he understands."

"Why did they do it?"

Behind them the monkey, who had been following them, said, "He had uncontrollable seizures."

"Did you?" the girl asked. She was watching a sea bird swooping low over the water and did not seem to care.

Nicholas picked up a shell and shied it at the monkey, who skipped out of the way. After half a minute's silence he said, "I had visions."

"Ooh, did you?"

"They didn't like that. They said I would fall down and jerk around horrible, and sometimes I guess I would hurt myself when I fell, and sometimes I'd bite my tongue and it would bleed. But that wasn't what it felt like to me; I wouldn't know about any of those things until afterward. To me it was like I had gone way far ahead, and I had to come back. I didn't want to."

The wind swayed Diane's hair, and she pushed it back from her face. "Did you see things that were going to happen?" she asked.

"Sometimes."

"Really? Did you?"

"Sometimes."

"Tell me about it. When you saw what was going to happen."

"I saw myself dead. I was all black and shrunk up like the dead stuff they cut off in the 'pontic gardens; and I was floating and turning, like in water but it wasn't water—just floating and turning out in space, in nothing. And there were lights on both sides of me, so both sides were bright but black, and I could see my teeth because the stuff"—he pulled at his cheeks—"had fallen off there, and they were really white."

"That hasn't happened yet."

"Not here."

"Tell me something you saw that happened."

"You mean, like somebody's sister was going to get married, don't you? That's what the girls where I was mostly wanted to know. Or were they going to go home; mostly it wasn't like that."

"But sometimes it was?"

"I guess."

"Tell me one."

Nicholas shook his head. "You wouldn't like it, and anyway it wasn't like that. Mostly it was lights like I never saw anyplace else, and voices like I never heard any other time, telling me things there aren't any words for; stuff like that, only now I can't ever go back. Listen, I wanted to ask you about Ignacio."

"He isn't anybody," the girl said.

"What do you mean, he isn't anybody? Is there anybody here besides you and me and Ignacio and Dr. Island?"

"Not that we can see or touch."

The monkey called, "There are other patients, but for the present, Nicholas, for your own well-being as well as theirs, it is best for you to remain by yourselves." It was a long sentence for a monkey.

"What's that about?"

"If I tell you, will you tell me about something you saw that really happened?"

"All right."

"Tell me first."

"There was this girl where I was—her name was Maya. They had, you know, boys' and girls' dorms, but you saw everybody in the rec room and the dining hall and so on, and she was in my psychodrama group." Her hair had been black, and shiny as the lacquered furniture in Dr. Hong's rooms, her skin white like the mother-of-pearl, her eyes long and narrow (making him think of cats' eyes) and darkly blue. She was fifteen, or so Nicholas believed—maybe sixteen. *I'm going home,* she told him. It was psychodrama, and he was her brother, younger than she, and she was already at home; but when she said this the floating ring of light that gave them the necessary separation from the small doctor-and-patient audience, ceased, by instant agreement, to be Maya's mother's living room and became a visiting lounge. Nicholas/Jerry said: "Hey, that's great! Hey, I got a new bike—when you come home you want to ride it?"

Maureen/Maya's mother said, "Maya, don't. You'll run into something and break your teeth, and you know how much they cost."

"You don't want me to have any fun."

"We do, dear, but *nice* fun. A girl has to be so much more careful—oh, Maya, I wish I could make you understand, really, how careful a girl has to be."

Nobody said anything, so Nicholas/Jerry filled in with, "It has a three-bladed prop, and I'm going to tape streamers to them with little weights at the ends, an' when I go down old thirty-seven B passageway, look out, here comes that old coleslaw grater!"

"Like this," Maya said, and held her legs together and extended her arms, to make a three-bladed bike prop or a crucifix. She had thrown herself into a spin as she made the movement, and revolved slowly, stage center—red shorts, white blouse, red shorts, white blouse, red shorts, no shoes.

Diane asked, "And you saw that she was never going home, she was going to hospital instead, she was going to cut her wrist there, she was going to die?"

Nicholas nodded.

"Did you tell her?"

"Yes," Nicholas said. "No."

"Make up your mind. Didn't you tell her? Now, don't get mad."

"Is it telling, when the one you tell doesn't understand?"

Diane thought about that for a few steps while Nicholas dashed water on the hot bruises Ignacio had left upon his face. "If it was plain and clear and she ought to have understood—that's the trouble I have with my family."

"What is?"

"They won't say things—do you know what I mean? I just

say look, just tell me, just tell me what I'm supposed to do, tell me what it is you want, but it's different all the time. My mother says, 'Diane, you ought to meet some boys, you can't go out with him, your father and I have never met him, we don't even know his family at all, Douglas, there's something I think you ought to know about Diane, she gets confused sometimes, we've had her to doctors, she's been in a hospital, try—' "

"Not to get her excited," Nicholas finished for her.

"Were you listening? I mean, are you from the Trojan Planets? Do you know my mother?"

"I only live in these places," Nicholas said, "that's for a long time. But you talk like other people."

"I feel better now that I'm with you; you're really nice. I wish you were older."

"I'm not sure I'm going to get much older."

"It's going to rain—feel it?"

Nicholas shook his head.

"Look." Diane jumped, bunnyrabbit-clumsy, three meters into the air. "See how high I can jump? That means people are sad and it's going to rain. I told you."

"No, you didn't."

"Yes, I did, Nicholas."

He waved the argument away, struck by a sudden thought. "You ever been to Callisto?"

The girl shook her head, and Nicholas said, "I have; that's where they did the operation. It's so big the gravity's mostly from natural mass, and it's all domed in, with a whole lot of air in it."

"So?"

"And when I was there it rained. There was a big trouble at one of the generating piles, and they shut it down and it got colder and colder until everybody in the hospital wore their blankets, just like Amerinds in books, and they locked the switches off on the heaters in the bathrooms, and the nurses and the comscreen told you all the time it wasn't dangerous, they were just rationing power to keep from blacking out the important stuff that was still running. And then it rained, just like on Earth. They said it got so cold the water condensed in the air, and it was like the whole hospital was right under a shower bath. Everybody on the top floor had to come down because it rained right on their beds, and for two nights I had a man in my room with me that had his arm cut off in a machine. But we couldn't jump any higher, and it got kind of dark."

"It doesn't always get dark here," Diane said. "Sometimes the rain sparkles. I think Dr. Island must do it to cheer everyone up."

"No," the waves explained, "or at least not in the way you mean, Diane."

Nicholas was hungry and started to ask them for something to eat, then turned his hunger in against itself, spat on the sand, and was still.

"It rains here when most of you are sad," the waves were saying, "because rain is a sad thing, to the human psyche. It is that, that sadness, perhaps because it recalls to unhappy people their own tears, that palliates melancholy."

Diane said, "Well, I know sometimes I feel better when it rains."

"That should help you to understand yourself. Most people are soothed when their environment is in harmony with their emotions, and anxious when it is not. An angry person becomes less angry in a red room, and unhappy people are only exasperated by sunshine and birdsong. Do you remember:

> "And, missing thee, I walk unseen
> On the dry smooth-shaven green
> To behold the wandering moon,
> Riding near her highest noon,

Like one that had been led astray
Through the heaven's wide pathless way?"

The girl shook her head.

Nicholas said, "No. Did somebody write that?" and then "You said you couldn't do anything."

The waves replied, "I can't—except talk to you."

"You make it rain."

"Your heart beats; I sense its pumping even as I speak—do you control the beating of your heart?"

"I can stop my breath."

"Can you stop your heart? Honestly, Nicholas?"

"I guess not."

"No more can I control the weather of my world, stop anyone from doing what he wishes, or feed you if you are hungry; with no need of volition on my part your emotions are monitored and averaged, and our weather responds. Calm and sunshine for tranquillity, rain for melancholy, storms for rage, and so on. This is what mankind has always wanted."

Diane asked, "What is?"

"That the environment should respond to human thought. That is the core of magic and the oldest dream of mankind; and here, on me, it is fact."

"So that we'll be well?"

Nicholas said angrily, "You're not sick!"

Dr. Island said, "So that some of you, at least, can return to society."

Nicholas threw a sea shell into the water as though to strike the mouth that spoke. "Why are we talking to this thing?"

"Wait, tot, I think it's interesting."

"Lies and lies."

Dr. Island said, "How do I lie, Nicholas?"

"You said it was magic—"

"No, I said that when humankind has dreamed of magic,

the wish behind that dream has been the omnipotence of thought. Have you never wanted to be a magician, Nicholas, making palaces spring up overnight, or riding an enchanted horse of ebony to battle with the demons of the air?"

"I am a magician—I have preternatural powers, and before they cut us in two—"

Diane interrupted him. "You said you averaged emotions. When you made it rain."

"Yes."

"Doesn't that mean that if one person was really, terribly sad, he'd move the average so much he could make it rain all by himself? Or whatever? That doesn't seem fair."

The waves might have smiled. "That has never happened. But if it did, Diane, if one person felt such deep emotion, think how great her need would be. Don't you think we should answer it?"

Diane looked at Nicholas, but he was walking again, his head swinging, ignoring her as well as the voice of the waves. "Wait," she called. "You said I wasn't sick; I am, you know."

"No, you're not."

She hurried after him. "Everyone says so, and sometimes I'm so confused, and other times I'm boiling inside, just boiling. Mum says if you've got something on the stove you don't want to have burn, you just have to keep one finger on the handle of the pan and it won't, but I can't, I can't always find the handle or remember."

Without looking back the boy said, "Your mother is probably sick; maybe your father too, I don't know. But you're not. If they'd just let you alone you'd be all right. Why shouldn't you get upset, having to live with two crazy people?"

"Nicholas!" She grabbed his thin shoulders. "That's not true!"

"Yes, it is."

"I am sick. Everyone says so."

"I don't; so 'everyone' just means the ones that do—isn't

that right? And if you don't either, that will be two; it can't be everyone then."

The girl called, "Doctor? Dr. Island?"

Nicholas said, "You aren't going to believe that, are you?"

"Dr. Island, is it true?"

"Is what true, Diane?"

"What he said. Am I sick?"

"Sickness—even physical illness—is relative, Diane; and complete health is an idealization, an abstraction, even if the other end of the scale is not."

"You know what I mean."

"You are not physically ill." A long, blue comber curled into a line of hissing spray reaching infinitely along the sea to their left and right. "As you said yourself a moment ago, you are sometimes confused, and sometimes disturbed."

"He said if it weren't for other people, if it weren't for my mother and father, I wouldn't have to be here."

"Diane . . ."

"Well, is that true or isn't it?"

"Most emotional illness would not exist, Diane, if it were possible in every case to separate oneself—in thought as well as circumstance—if only for a time."

"Separate oneself?"

"Did you ever think of going away, at least for a time?"

The girl nodded, then as though she were not certain Dr. Island could see her, said, "Often, I suppose; leaving the school and getting my own compartment somewhere—going to Achilles. Sometimes I wanted to so badly."

"Why didn't you?"

"They would have worried. And anyway, they would have found me, and made me come home."

"Would it have done any good if I—or a human doctor—had told them not to?"

When the girl said nothing Nicholas snapped, "You could have locked them up."

"They were functioning, Nicholas. They bought and sold; they worked, and paid their taxes—"

Diane said softly, "It wouldn't have done any good anyway, Nicholas; they are inside me."

"Diane was no longer functioning: she was failing every subject at the university she attended, and her presence in her classes, when she came, disturbed the instructors and the other students. You were not functioning either, and people of your own age were afraid of you."

"That's what counts with you, then. Functioning."

"If I were different from the world, would that help you when you got back into the world?"

"You are different." Nicholas kicked the sand. "Nobody ever saw a place like this."

"You mean that reality to you is metal corridors, rooms without windows, noise."

"Yes."

"That is the unreality, Nicholas. Most people have never had to endure such things. Even now, this—my beach, my sea, my trees—is more in harmony with most human lives than your metal corridors; and here, I am your social environment—what individuals call 'they.' You see, sometimes if we take people who are troubled back to something like me, to an idealized natural setting, it helps them."

"Come on," Nicholas told the girl. He took her arm, acutely conscious of being so much shorter than she.

"A question," murmured the waves. "If Diane's parents had been taken here instead of Diane, do you think it would have helped them?"

Nicholas did not reply.

"We have treatments for disturbed persons, Nicholas. But, at least for the time being, we have no treatment for disturbing persons." Diane and the boy had turned away, and the waves' hissing and slapping ceased to be speech. Gulls wheeled overhead, and once a red-and-yellow parrot fluttered from one palm to another. A monkey running on all fours like a little dog approached them, and Nicholas chased it, but it escaped.

"I'm going to take one of those things apart someday," he said, "and pull the wires out."

"Are we going to walk all the way 'round?" Diane asked. She might have been talking to herself.

"Can you do that?"

"Oh, you can't walk all around Dr. Island; it would be too long, and you can't get there anyway. But we could walk until we get back to where we started—we're probably more than halfway now."

"Are there other islands you can't see from here?"

The girl shook her head. "I don't think so; there's just this one big island in this satellite, and all the rest is water."

"Then if there's only the one island, we're going to have to walk all around it to get back to where we started. What are you laughing at?"

"Look down the beach, as far as you can. Never mind how it slips off to the side—pretend it's straight."

"I don't see anything."

"Don't you? Watch." Diane leaped into the air, six meters or more this time, and waved her arms.

"It looks like there's somebody ahead of us, way down the beach."

"Uh-huh. Now look behind."

"Okay, there's somebody there too. Come to think of it, I saw someone on the beach when I first got here. It seemed funny to see so far, but I guess I thought they were other patients. Now I see two people."

"They're us. That was probably yourself you saw the other time, too. There are just so many of us to each strip of beach, and Dr. Island only wants certain ones to mix. So the space bends around. When we get to one end of our strip and try to step over, we'll be at the other end."

"How did you find out?"

"Dr. Island told me about it when I first came here." The girl was silent for a moment, and her smile vanished. "Listen, Nicholas, do you want to see something really funny?"

Nicholas asked, "What?" As he spoke, a drop of rain struck his face.

"You'll see. Come on, though. We have to go into the middle instead of following the beach, and it will give us a chance to get under the trees and out of the rain."

When they had left the sand and the sound of the surf, and were walking on solid ground under green-leaved trees, Nicholas said, "Maybe we can find some fruit." They were so light now that he had to be careful not to bound into the air with each step. The rain fell slowly around them, in crystal spheres.

"Maybe," the girl said doubtfully. "Wait, let's stop here." She sat down where a huge tree sent twenty-meter wooden arches over dark, mossy ground. "Want to climb up there and see if you can find us something?"

"All right," Nicholas agreed. He jumped, and easily caught hold of a branch far above the girl's head. In a moment he was climbing in a green world, with the rain pattering all around him; he followed narrowing limbs into leafy wildernesses where the cool water ran from every twig he touched, and twice found the empty nests of birds, and once a slender snake, green as any leaf with a head as long as his thumb; but there was no fruit. "Nothing," he said, when he dropped down beside the girl once more.

"That's all right, we'll find something."

He said, "I hope so," and noticed that she was looking at him oddly, then realized that his left hand had lifted itself to touch her right breast. It dropped as he looked, and he felt his face grow hot. He said, "I'm sorry."

"That's all right."

"We like you. He—over there—he can't talk, you see. I guess I can't talk either."

"I think it's just you—in two pieces. I don't care."

"Thanks." He had picked up a leaf, dead and damp, and was tearing it to shreds; first his right hand tearing while the left held the leaf, then turnabout. "Where does the rain come from?" The dirty flakes clung to the fingers of both.

"Hmm?"

"Where does the rain come from? I mean, it isn't because it's colder here now, like on Callisto; it's because the gravity's turned down some way, isn't it?"

"From the sea. Don't you know how this place is built?" Nicholas shook his head.

"Didn't they show it to you from the ship when you came? It's beautiful. They showed it to me—I just sat there and looked at it, and I wouldn't talk to them, and the nurse thought I wasn't paying any attention, but I heard everything. I just didn't want to talk to her. It wasn't any use."

"I know how you felt."

"But they didn't show it to you?"

"No, on my ship they kept me locked up because I burned some stuff. They thought I couldn't start a fire without an igniter, but if you have electricity in the wall sockets it's easy. They had a thing on me—you know?" He clasped his arms to his body to show how he had been restrained. "I bit one of them, too—I guess I didn't tell you that yet: I bite people. They locked me up, and for a long time I had nothing to do, and then I could feel us dock with something, and they came and got me and pulled me down a regular companionway for a long time, and it just seemed like a regular place. Then they stuck me full of Tranquil-C—I guess they didn't know it doesn't hardly work on me at all—with a pneumogun, and lifted a kind of door thing and shoved me up."

"Didn't they make you undress?"

"I already was. When they put the ties on me I did things in my clothes and they had to take them off me. It made them mad." He grinned unevenly. "Does Tranquil-C work on you? Or any of that other stuff?"

"I suppose they would, but then I never do the sort of thing you do anyway."

"Maybe you ought to."

"Sometimes they used to give me medication that was supposed to cheer me up; then I couldn't sleep, and I walked and walked, you know, and ran into things and made a lot of trouble for everyone; but what good does it do?"

Nicholas shrugged. "Not doing it doesn't do any good either—I mean, we're both here. My way, I know I've made them jump; they shoot that stuff in me and I'm not mad any more, but I know what it is and I just think what I would do if I *were* mad, and I do it, and when it wears off I'm glad I did."

"I think you're still angry somewhere, deep down."

Nicholas was already thinking of something else. "This island says Ignacio kills people." He paused. "What does it look like?"

"Ignacio?"

"No, I've seen him. Dr. Island."

"Oh, you mean when I was in the ship. The satellite's round of course, and all clear except where Dr. Island is, so that's a dark spot. The rest of it's temperglass, and from space you can't even see the water."

"That *is* the sea up there, isn't it?" Nicholas asked, trying to look up at it through the tree leaves and the rain. "I thought it was when I first came."

"Sure. It's like a glass ball, and we're inside, and the water's inside too, and just goes all around up the curve."

"That's why I could see so far out on the beach, isn't it? Instead of dropping down from you like on Callisto it bends up so you can see it."

The girl nodded. "And the water lets the light through, but filters out the ultraviolet. Besides, it gives us thermal mass, so we don't heat up too much when we're between the sun and the Bright Spot."

"Is that what keeps us warm? The Bright Spot?"

Diane nodded again. "We go around in ten hours, you see, and that holds us over it all the time."

"Why can't I see it, then? It ought to look like Sol does from the Belt, only bigger; but there's just a shimmer in the sky, even when it's not raining."

"The waves diffract the light and break up the image. You'd see the Focus, though, if the air weren't so clear. Do you know what the Focus is?"

Nicholas shook his head.

"We'll get to it pretty soon, after this rain stops. Then I'll tell you."

"I still don't understand about the rain."

Unexpectedly Diane giggled. "I just thought—do you know what I was supposed to be? While I was going to school?"

"Quiet," Nicholas said.

"No, silly. I mean what I was being trained to do, if I graduated and all that. I was going to be a teacher, with all those cameras on me and tots from everywhere watching and popping questions on the two-way. Jolly time. Now I'm doing it here, only there's no one but you."

"You mind?"

"No, I suppose I enjoy it." There was a black-and-blue mark on Diane's thigh, and she rubbed it pensively with one hand as she spoke. "Anyway, there are three ways to make gravity. Do you know them? Answer, clerk."

"Sure; acceleration, mass, and synthesis."

"That's right; motion and mass are both bendings of space, of course, which is why Zeno's paradox doesn't work out that way, and why masses move toward each other—what we call falling—or at least try to; and if they're held apart it produces the tension we perceive as a force and call weight and all that rot. So naturally if you bend the space direct, you synthesize a gravity effect, and that's what holds all that water up against the translucent shell—there's nothing like enough mass to do it by itself."

"You mean"—Nicholas held out his hand to catch a slow-moving globe of rain—"that this is water from the sea?"

"Right-o, up on top. Do you see, the temperature differences in the air make the winds, and the winds make the waves and surf you saw when we were walking along the shore. When the waves break they throw up these little drops, and if you watch you'll see that even when it's clear they go up a long way sometimes. Then if the gravity is less they can get away altogether, and if we were on the outside they'd fly off into space; but we aren't, we're inside, so all they can do is go across the center, more or less, until they hit the water again, or Dr. Island."

"Dr. Island said they had storms sometimes, when people got mad."

"Yes. Lots of wind, and so there's lots of rain too. Only the rain then is because the wind tears the tops off the waves, and you don't get light like you do in a normal rain."

"What makes so much wind?"

"I don't know. It happens somehow."

They sat in silence, Nicholas listening to the dripping of the leaves. He remembered then that they had spun the hospital module, finally, to get the little spheres of clotting blood out of the air; Maya's blood was building up on the grills of the purification intake ducts, spotting them black, and someone had been afraid they would decay there and smell. He had not been there when they did it, but he could imagine the droplets settling, like this, in the slow spin. The old psycho-drama group had already been broken up, and when he saw Maureen or any of the others in the rec room they talked about Good Old Days. It had not seemed like Good Old Days then except that Maya had been there.

Diane said, "It's going to stop."

"It looks just as bad to me."

"No, it's going to stop—see, they're falling a little faster now, and I feel heavier."

Nicholas stood up. "You rested enough yet? You want to go on?"

"We'll get wet."

He shrugged.

"I don't want to get my hair wet, Nicholas. It'll be over in a minute."

He sat down again. "How long have you been here?"

"I'm not sure."

"Don't you count the days?"

"I lose track a lot."

"Longer than a week?"

"Nicholas, don't ask me, all right?"

"Isn't there anybody on this piece of Dr. Island except you and me and Ignacio?"

"I don't think there was anyone but Ignacio before you came."

"Who is he?"

She looked at him.

"Well, who is he? You know me—us—Nicholas Kenneth de Vore; and you're Diane who?"

"Phillips."

"And you're from the Trojan Planets, and I was from the Outer Belt, I guess, to start with. What about Ignacio? You talk to him sometimes, don't you? Who is he?"

"I don't know. He's important."

For an instant, Nicholas froze. "What does that mean?"

"Important." The girl was feeling her knees, running her hands back and forth across them.

"Maybe everybody's important."

"I know you're just a tot, Nicholas, but don't be so stupid. Come on, you wanted to go, let's go now. It's pretty well stopped." She stood, stretching her thin body, her arms over her head. "My knees are rough—you made me think of that.

When I came here they were still so smooth, I think. I used to put a certain lotion on them. Because my Dad would feel them, and my hands and elbows too, and he'd say if they weren't smooth nobody'd ever want me; Mum wouldn't say anything, but she'd be cross after, and they used to come and visit, and so I kept a bottle in my room and I used to put it on. Once I drank some."

Nicholas was silent.

"Aren't you going to ask me if I died?" She stepped ahead of him, pulling aside the dripping branches. "See here, I'm sorry I said you were stupid."

"I'm just thinking," Nicholas said. "I'm not mad at you. Do you really know anything about him?"

"No, but look at it." She gestured. "Look around you; someone *built* all this."

"You mean it cost a lot."

"It's automated, of course, but still . . . well, the other places where you were before—how much space was there for each patient? Take the total volume and divide it by the number of people there."

"Okay, this is a whole lot bigger, but maybe they think we're worth it."

"Nicholas . . ." She paused. "Nicholas, Ignacio is homicidal. Didn't Dr. Island tell you?"

"Yes."

"And you're fourteen and not very big for it, and I'm a girl. Who are they worried about?"

The look on Nicholas's face startled her.

After an hour or more of walking they came to it. It was a band of withered vegetation, brown and black and tumbling, and as straight as if it had been drawn with a ruler. "I was afraid it wasn't going to be here," Diane said. "It moves around whenever there's a storm. It might not have been in our sector any more at all."

Nicholas asked, "What is it?"

"The Focus. It's been all over, but mostly the plants grow back quickly when it's gone."

"It smells funny—like the kitchen in a place where they wanted me to work in the kitchen once."

"Vegetables rotting, that's what that is. What did you do?"

"Nothing—put detergent in the stuff they were cooking. What makes this?"

"The Bright Spot. See, when it's just about overhead the curve of the sky and the water up there make a lens. It isn't a very good lens—a lot of the light scatters. But enough is focused to do this. It wouldn't fry us if it came past right now, if that's what you're wondering, because it's not that hot. I've stood right in it, but you want to get out in a minute."

"I thought it was going to be about seeing ourselves down the beach."

Diane seated herself on the trunk of a fallen tree. "It was, really. The last time I was here it was further from the water, and I suppose it had been there a long time, because it had cleared out a lot of the dead stuff. The sides of the sector are nearer here, you see; the whole sector narrows down like a piece of pie. So you could look down the Focus either way and see yourself nearer than you could on the beach. It was almost as if you were in a big, big room, with a looking-glass on each wall, or as if you could stand behind yourself. I thought you might like it."

"I'm going to try it here," Nicholas announced, and he clambered up one of the dead trees while the girl waited below, but the dry limbs creaked and snapped beneath his feet, and he could not get high enough to see himself in either direction. When he dropped to the ground beside her again, he said, "There's nothing to eat here either, is there?"

"I haven't found anything."

"They—I mean, Dr. Island wouldn't just let us starve, would he?"

"I don't think he could do anything; that's the way this place is built. Sometimes you find things, and I've tried to catch fish, but I never could. A couple of times Ignacio gave me part of what he had, though; he's good at it. I bet you think I'm skinny, don't you? But I was a lot fatter when I came here."

"What are we going to do now?"

"Keep walking, I suppose, Nicholas. Maybe go back to the water."

"Do you think we'll find anything?"

From a decaying log, insect stridulations called, "Wait."

Nicholas asked, "Do *you* know where anything is?"

"Something for you to eat? Not at present. But I can show you something much more interesting, not far from here, than this clutter of dying trees. Would you like to see it?"

Diane said, "Don't go, Nicholas."

"What is it?"

"Diane, who calls this 'the Focus,' calls what I wish to show you 'the Point.' "

Nicholas asked Diane, "Why shouldn't I go?"

"I'm not going. I went there once anyway."

"I took her," Dr. Island said. "And I'll take you. I wouldn't take you if I didn't think it might help you."

"I don't think Diane liked it."

"Diane may not wish to be helped—help may be painful, and often people do not. But it is my business to help them if I can, whether or not they wish it."

"Suppose I don't want to go?"

"Then I cannot compel you; you know that. But you will be the only patient in this sector who has not seen it, Nicholas, as well as the youngest; both Diane and Ignacio have, and Ignacio goes there often."

"Is it dangerous?"

"No. Are you afraid?"

Nicholas looked questioningly at Diane. "What is it? What will I see?"

She had walked away while he was talking to Dr. Island, and was now sitting cross-legged on the ground about five meters from where Nicholas stood, staring at her hands. Nicholas repeated, "What will I see, Diane?" He did not think she would answer.

She said, "A glass. A mirror."

"Just a mirror?"

"You know how I told you to climb the tree here? The Point is where the edges come together. You can see yourself —like on the beach—but closer."

Nicholas was disappointed. "I've seen myself in mirrors lots of times."

Dr. Island, whose voice was now in the sighing of the dead leaves, whispered, "Did you have a mirror in your room, Nicholas, before you came here?"

"A steel one."

"So that you could not break it?"

"I guess so. I threw things at it sometimes, but it just got puckers in it." Remembering dimpled reflections, Nicholas laughed.

"You can't break this one either."

"It doesn't sound like it's worth going to see."

"I think it is."

"Diane, do you still think I shouldn't go?"

There was no reply. The girl sat staring at the ground in front of her. Nicholas walked over to look at her and found a tear had washed a damp trail down each thin cheek, but she did not move when he touched her. "She's catatonic, isn't she," he said.

A green limb just outside the Focus nodded. "Catatonic schizophrenia."

"I had a doctor once that said those names—like that. They didn't mean anything." (The doctor had been a therapy robot, but a human doctor gave more status. Robots' patients sat in doorless booths—two and a half hours a day for Nicholas: an hour and a half in the morning, an hour in the afternoon—and talked to something that appeared to be a small, friendly food freezer. Some people sat every day in silence, while others talked continually, and for such patients as these the attendants seldom troubled to turn the machines on.)

"He meant cause and treatment. He was correct."

Nicholas stood looking down at the girl's streaked, brown-blond head. "What *is* the cause? I mean for her."

"I don't know."

"And what's the treatment?"

"You are seeing it."

"Will it help her?"

"Probably not."

"Listen, she can hear you, don't you know that? She hears everything we say."

"If my answer disturbs you, Nicholas, I can change it. It will help her if she wants to be helped; if she insists on clasping her illness to her it will not."

"We ought to go away from here," Nicholas said uneasily.

"To your left you will see a little path, a very faint one. Between the twisted tree and the bush with the yellow flowers."

Nicholas nodded and began to walk, looking back at Diane several times. The flowers were butterflies, who fled in a cloud of color when he approached them, and he wondered if Dr. Island had known. When he had gone a hundred paces and was well away from the brown and rotting vegetation, he said, "She was sitting in the Focus."

"Yes."

"Is she still there?"

"Yes."

"What will happen when the Bright Spot comes?"

"Diane will become uncomfortable and move, if she is still there."

"Once in one of the places I was in there was a man who was like that, and they said he wouldn't get anything to eat if he didn't get up and get it, they weren't going to feed him with the nose tube any more; and they didn't, and he died. We told them about it and they wouldn't do anything and he starved to death right there, and when he was dead they rolled him off onto a stretcher and changed the bed and put somebody else there."

"I know, Nicholas. You told the doctors at St. John's about all that, and it is in your file; but think: well men have starved themselves—yes, to death—to protest what they felt were political injustices. Is it so surprising that your friend killed himself in the same way to protest what he felt as a psychic injustice?"

"He wasn't my friend. Listen, did you really mean it when you said the treatment she was getting here would help Diane if she wanted to be helped?"

"No."

Nicholas halted in mid-stride. "You didn't mean it? You don't think it's true?"

"No. I doubt that anything will help her."

"I don't think you ought to lie to us."

"Why not? If by chance you become well you will be released, and if you are released you will have to deal with your society, which will lie to you frequently. Here, where there are so few individuals, I must take the place of society. I have explained that."

"Is that what you are?"

"Society's surrogate? Of course. Who do you imagine built me? What else could I be?"

"The doctor."

"You have had many doctors, and so has she. Not one of them has benefited you much."

"I'm not sure you even want to help us."

"Do you wish to see what Diane calls 'the Point'?"

"I guess so."

"Then you must walk. You will not see it standing here."

Nicholas walked, thrusting aside leafy branches and dangling creepers wet with rain. The jungle smelled of the life of green things; there were ants on the tree trunks, and dragonflies with hot, red bodies and wings as long as his hands. "Do you want to help us?" he asked after a time.

"My feelings toward you are ambivalent. But when you wish to be helped, I wish to help you."

The ground sloped gently upward, and as it rose became somewhat more clear, the big trees a trifle farther apart, the underbrush spent in grass and fern. Occasionally there were stone outcrops to be climbed, and clearings open to the tumbling sky. Nicholas asked, "Who made this trail?"

"Ignacio. He comes here often."

"He's not afraid, then? Diane's afraid."

"Ignacio is afraid too, but he comes."

"Diane says Ignacio is important."

"Yes."

"What do you mean by that? Is he important? More important than we are?"

"Do you remember that I told you I was the surrogate of society? What do you think society wants, Nicholas?"

"Everybody to do what it says."

"You mean conformity. Yes, there must be conformity, but something else too—consciousness."

"I don't want to hear about it."

"Without consciousness, which you may call sensitivity if you are careful not to allow yourself to be confused by the term, there is no progress. A century ago, Nicholas, mankind was suffocating on Earth; now it is suffocating again. About half of the people who have contributed substantially to the advance of humanity have shown signs of emotional disturbance."

"I told you, I don't want to hear about it. I asked you an easy question—is Ignacio more important than Diane and me—and you won't tell me. I've heard all this you're saying.

I've heard it fifty, maybe a hundred times from everybody, and it's lies; it's the regular thing, and you've got it written down on a card somewhere to read out when anybody asks. Those people you talk about that went crazy, they went crazy because while they were 'advancing humanity,' or whatever you call it, people kicked them out of their rooms because they couldn't pay, and while they were getting thrown out you were making other people rich that had never done anything in their whole lives except think about how to get that way."

"Sometimes it is hard, Nicholas, to determine before the fact—or even at the time—just who should be honored."

"How do you know if you've never tried?"

"You asked if Ignacio was more important than Diane or yourself. I can only say that Ignacio seems to me to hold a brighter promise of a full recovery coupled with a substantial contribution to human progress."

"If he's so good, why did he crack up?"

"Many do, Nicholas. Even among the inner planets space is not a kind environment for mankind; and our space, trans-Martian space, is worse. Any young person here, anyone like yourself or Diane who would seem to have a better-than-average chance of adapting to the conditions we face, is precious."

"Or Ignacio."

"Yes, or Ignacio. Ignacio has a tested IQ of two hundred and ten, Nicholas. Diane's is one hundred and twenty. Your own is ninety-five."

"They never took mine."

"It's on your records, Nicholas."

"They tried to and I threw down the helmet and it broke; Sister Carmela—she was the nurse—just wrote down something on the paper and sent me back."

"I see. I will ask for a complete investigation of this, Nicholas."

"Sure."

"Don't you believe me?"

"I don't think you believed me."

"Nicholas, Nicholas . . ." The long tongues of grass now beginning to appear beneath the immense trees sighed. "Can't you see that a certain measure of trust between the two of us is essential?"

"Did you believe me?"

"Why do you ask? Suppose I were to say I did; would you believe that?"

"When you told me I had been reclassified."

"You would have to be retested, for which there are no facilities here."

"If you believed me, why did you say retested? I told you I haven't ever been tested at all—but anyway you could cross out the ninety-five."

"It is impossible for me to plan your therapy without some estimate of your intelligence, Nicholas, and I have nothing with which to replace it."

The ground was sloping up more sharply now, and in a clearing the boy halted and turned to look back at the leafy film, like algae over a pool, beneath which he had climbed, and at the sea beyond. To his right and left his view was still hemmed with foliage, and ahead of him a meadow on edge (like the square of sand through which he had come, though he did not think of that), dotted still with trees, stretched steeply toward an invisible summit. It seemed to him that under his feet the mountainside swayed ever so slightly. Abruptly he demanded of the wind, "Where's Ignacio?"

"Not here. Much closer to the beach."

"And Diane?"

"Where you left her. Do you enjoy the panorama?"

"It's pretty, but it feels like we're rocking."

"We are. I am moored to the temperglass exterior of our satellite by two hundred cables, but the tide and the currents none the less impart a slight motion to my body. Naturally this movement is magnified as you go higher."

"I thought you were fastened right onto the hull; if there's water under you, how do people get in and out?"

"I am linked to the main air lock by a communication tube. To you when you came, it probably seemed an ordinary companionway."

Nicholas nodded and turned his back on leaves and sea and began to climb again.

"You are in a beautiful spot, Nicholas; do you open your heart to beauty?" After waiting for an answer that did not come, the wind sang:

> "The mountain wooded to the peak, the lawns
> And winding glades high up like ways to Heaven,
> The slender coco's drooping crown of plumes,
> The lightning flash of insect and of bird,
> The lustre of the long convolvuluses
> That coil'd around the stately stems, and ran
> Ev'n to the limit of the land, the glows
> And glories of the broad belt of the world,
> All these he saw."

"Does this mean nothing to you, Nicholas?"

"You read a lot, don't you?"

"Often, when it is dark, everyone else is asleep and there is very little else for me to do."

"You talk like a woman; are you a woman?"

"How could I be a woman?"

"You know what I mean. Except, when you were talking mostly to Diane, you sounded more like a man."

"You haven't yet said you think me beautiful."

"You're an Easter egg."

"What do you mean by that, Nicholas?"

"Never mind." He saw the egg as it had hung in the air before him, shining with gold and covered with flowers.

"Eggs are dyed with pretty colors for Easter, and my colors are beautiful—is that what you mean, Nicholas?"

His mother had brought the egg on visiting day, but she could never have made it. Nicholas knew who must have made it. The gold was that very pure gold used for shielding delicate instruments; the clear flakes of crystallized carbon that dotted the egg's surface with tiny stars could only have come from a laboratory high-pressure furnace. How angry he must have been when she told him she was going to give it to him.

"It's pretty, isn't it, Nicky?"

It hung in the weightlessness between them, turning very slowly with the memory of her scented gloves.

"The flowers are meadowsweet, fraxinella, lily of the valley, and moss rose—though I wouldn't expect you to recognize them, darling." His mother had never been below the orbit of Mars, but she pretended to have spent her girlhood on Earth; each reference to the lie filled Nicholas with inexpressible fury and shame. The egg was about twenty centimeters long and it revolved, end over end, in some small fraction more than eight of the pulse beats he felt in his cheeks. Visiting time had twenty-three minutes to go.

"Aren't you going to look at it?"

"I can see it from here." He tried to make her understand. "I can see every part of it. The little red things are aluminum oxide crystals, right?"

"I mean, look *inside*, Nicky."

He saw then that there was a lens at one end, disguised as a dewdrop in the throat of an asphodel. Gently he took the egg in his hands, closed one eye, and looked. The light of the interior was not, as he had half expected, gold tinted, but brilliantly white, deriving from some concealed source. A world surely meant for Earth shone within, as though seen from below the orbit of the moon—indigo sea and emerald land. Rivers brown and clear as tea ran down long plains.

His mother said, "Isn't it pretty?"

Night hung at the corners in funereal purple, and sent long shadows like cold and lovely arms to caress the day; and while he watched and it fell, long-necked birds of so dark a pink that they were nearly red trailed stilt legs across the sky, their wings making crosses.

"They are called flamingos," Dr. Island said, following the direction of his eyes. "Isn't it a pretty word? For a pretty bird, but I don't think we'd like them as much if we called them sparrows, would we?"

His mother said, "I'm going to take it home and keep it for you. It's too nice to leave with a little boy, but if you ever come home again it will be waiting for you. On your dresser, beside your hairbrushes."

Nicholas said, "Words just mix you up."

"You shouldn't despise them, Nicholas. Besides having great beauty of their own, they are useful in reducing tension. You might benefit from that."

"You mean you talk yourself out of it."

"I mean that a person's ability to verbalize his feelings, if only to himself, may prevent them from destroying him. Evolution teaches us, Nicholas, that the original purpose of language was to ritualize men's threats and curses, his spells to compel the gods; communication came later. Words can be a safety valve."

Nicholas said, "I want to be a bomb; a bomb doesn't need a safety valve." To his mother, "Is that South America, Mama?"

"No, dear, India. The Malabar Coast on your left, the Coromandel Coast on your right, and Ceylon below." Words.

"A bomb destroys itself, Nicholas."

"A bomb doesn't care."

He was climbing resolutely now, his toes grabbing at tree roots and the soft, mossy soil; his physician was no longer the wind but a small brown monkey that followed a stone's throw behind him. "I hear someone coming," he said.

"Yes."

"Is it Ignacio?"

"No, it is Nicholas. You are close now."

"Close to the Point?"

"Yes."

He stopped and looked around him. The sounds he had heard, the naked feet padding on soft ground, stopped as well. Nothing seemed strange; the land still rose, and there were large trees, widely spaced, with moss growing in their deepest shade, grass where there was more light. "The three big trees," Nicholas said, "they're just alike. Is that how you know where we are?"

"Yes."

In his mind he called the one before him "Ceylon"; the others were "Coromandel" and "Malabar." He walked toward Ceylon, studying its massive, twisted limbs; a boy naked as himself walked out of the forest to his left, toward Malabar—this boy was not looking at Nicholas, who shouted and ran toward him.

The boy disappeared. Only Malabar, solid and real, stood before Nicholas; he ran to it, touched its rough bark with his hand, and then saw beyond it a fourth tree, similar too to the Ceylon tree, around which a boy peered with averted head. Nicholas watched him for a moment, then said, "I see."

"Do you?" the monkey chattered.

"It's like a mirror, only backwards. The light from the front of me goes out and hits the edge, and comes in the other side, only I can't see it because I'm not looking that way. What I see is the light from my back, sort of, because it comes back this way. When I ran, did I get turned around?"

"Yes, you ran out the left side of the segment, and of course returned immediately from the right."

"I'm not scared. It's kind of fun." He picked up a stick and threw it as hard as he could toward the Malabar tree. It vanished, whizzed over his head, vanished again, slapped the back of his legs. "Did this scare Diane?"

There was no answer. He strode farther, palely naked boys walking to his left and right, but always looking away from him, gradually coming closer.

"Don't go farther," Dr. Island said behind him. "It can be dangerous if you try to pass through the Point itself."

"I see it," Nicholas said. He saw three more trees, growing very close together, just ahead of him; their branches seemed strangely intertwined as they danced together in the wind, and beyond them there was nothing at all.

"You can't actually go through the Point," Dr. Island Monkey said. "The tree covers it."

"Then why did you warn me about it?" Limping and scarred, the boys to his right and left were no more than two meters away now; he had discovered that if he looked straight ahead he could sometimes glimpse their bruised profiles.

"That's far enough, Nicholas."

"I want to touch the tree."

He took another step, and another, then turned. The Malabar boy turned too, presenting his narrow back, on which the ribs and spine seemed welts. Nicholas reached out both arms and laid his hands on the thin shoulders, and as he did, felt other hands—the cool, unfeeling hands of a stranger, dry hands too small—touch his own shoulders and creep upward toward his neck.

"Nicholas!"

He jumped sidewise away from the tree and looked at his hands, his head swaying. "It wasn't me."

"Yes, it was, Nicholas," the monkey said.

"It was one of them."

"You are all of them."

In one quick motion Nicholas snatched up an arm-long section of fallen limb and hurled it at the monkey. It struck the little creature, knocking it down, but the monkey sprang up and fled on three legs. Nicholas sprinted after it.

He had nearly caught it when it darted to one side; as quickly, he turned toward the other, springing for the monkey he saw running toward him there. In an instant it was in his grip, feebly trying to bite. He slammed its head against the ground, then catching it by the ankles swung it against the Ceylon tree until at the third impact he heard the skull crack, and stopped.

He had expected wires, but there were none. Blood oozed from the battered little face, and the furry body was warm and limp in his hands. Leaves above his head said, "You haven't killed me, Nicholas. You never will."

"How does it work?" He was still searching for wires, tiny circuit cards holding micro-logic. He looked about for a sharp stone with which to open the monkey's body, but could find none.

"It is just a monkey," the leaves said. "If you had asked, I would have told you."

"How did you make him talk?" He dropped the monkey, stared at it for a moment, then kicked it. His fingers were bloody, and he wiped them on the leaves of the tree.

"Only my mind speaks to yours, Nicholas."

"Oh," he said. And then, "I've heard of that. I didn't think it would be like this. I thought it would be in my head."

"Your record shows no auditory hallucinations, but haven't you ever known someone who had them?"

"I knew a girl once . . ." He paused.

"Yes?"

"She twisted noises—you know?"

"Yes."

"Like, it would just be a service cart out in the corridor, but she'd hear the fan, and think . . ."

"What?"

"Oh, different things. That it was somebody talking, calling her."

"Hear them?"

"What?" He sat up in his bunk. "Maya?"

"They're coming after me."

"Maya?"

Dr. Island, through the leaves, said, "When I talk to you, Nicholas, your mind makes any sound you hear the vehicle for my thoughts' content. You may hear me softly in the patter of rain, or joyfully in the singing of a bird—but if I wished I could amplify what I say until every idea and suggestion I wished to give would be driven like a nail into your consciousness. Then you would do whatever I wished you to."

"I don't believe it," Nicholas said. "If you can do that, why don't you tell Diane not to be catatonic?"

"First, because she might retreat more deeply into her disease in an effort to escape me; and second, because ending her catatonia in that way would not remove its cause."

"And thirdly?"

"I did not say 'thirdly,' Nicholas."

"I thought I heard it—when two leaves touched."

"Thirdly, Nicholas, because both you and she have been chosen for your effect on someone else; if I were to change her—or you—so abruptly, that effect would be lost." Dr. Island was a monkey again now, a new monkey that chattered from the protection of a tree twenty meters away. Nicholas threw a stick at him.

"The monkeys are only little animals, Nicholas; they like to follow people, and they chatter."

"I bet Ignacio kills them."

"No, he likes them; he only kills fish to eat."

Nicholas was suddenly aware of his hunger. He began to walk.

He found Ignacio on the beach, praying. For an hour or more, Nicholas hid behind the trunk of a palm watching him, but for a long time he could not decide to whom Ignacio prayed. He was kneeling just where the lacy edges of the breakers died, looking out toward the water; and from time to time he bowed, touching his forehead to the damp sand; then Nicholas could hear his voice, faintly, over the crashing and hissing of the waves. In general, Nicholas approved of prayer, having observed that those who prayed were usually more interesting companions than those who did not; but he had also noticed that though it made no difference what name the devotee gave the object of his devotions, it was important to discover how the god was conceived. Ignacio did not seem to be praying to Dr. Island—he would, Nicholas thought, have been facing the other way for that—and for a time he wondered if he were not praying to the waves. From his position behind him he followed Ignacio's line of vision out and out, wave upon wave into the bright, confused sky, up and up until at last it curved completely around and came to rest on Ignacio's back again; and then it occurred to him that Ignacio might be praying to himself. He left the palm trunk then and walked about halfway to the place where Ignacio knelt, and sat down. Above the sounds of the sea and the murmuring of Ignacio's voice hung a silence so immense and fragile that it seemed that at any moment the entire crystal satellite might ring like a gong.

After a time Nicholas felt his left side trembling. With his right hand he began to stroke it, running his fingers down his left arm, and from his left shoulder to the thigh. It worried him that his left side should be so frightened, and he wondered if perhaps that other half of his brain, from which he was forever severed, could hear what Ignacio was saying to the waves. He began to pray himself, so that the other (and perhaps Ignacio too) could hear, saying not quite beneath his breath, "Don't worry, don't be afraid, he's not going to hurt us, he's nice, and if he does we'll get him; we're only going to get something to eat, maybe he'll show us how to catch fish, I think he'll be nice this time." But he knew, or at least felt he knew, that Ignacio would not be nice this time.

Eventually Ignacio stood up; he did not turn to face Nicholas, but waded out to sea; then, as though he had known Nicholas was behind him all the time (though Nicholas was not sure he had been heard—perhaps, so he thought, Dr. Island had told Ignacio), he gestured to indicate that Nicholas should follow him.

The water was colder than he remembered, the sand coarse and gritty between his toes. He thought of what Dr. Island had told him—about floating—and that a part of her must be this sand, under the water, reaching out (how far?) into the sea; when she ended there would be nothing but the clear temperglass of the satellite itself, far down.

"Come," Ignacio said. "Can you swim?" Just as though he had forgotten the night before. Nicholas said yes, he could, wondering if Ignacio would look around at him when he spoke. He did not.

"And do you know why you are here?"

"You told me to come."

"Ignacio means *here*. Does this not remind you of any place you have seen before, little one?"

Nicholas thought of the crystal grong and the Easter egg, then of the micro-thin globes of perfumed vapor that, at home, were sometimes sent floating down the corridors at Christmas to explode in clean dust and a cold smell of pine forests when the children struck them with their hopping-canes; but he said nothing.

Ignacio continued, "Let Ignacio tell you a story. Once there was a man—a boy, actually—on the Earth, who—"

Nicholas wondered why it was always men (most often doctors and clinical psychologists, in his experience) who wanted to tell you stories. Jesus, he recalled, was always telling everyone stories, and the Virgin Mary almost never, though a woman he had once known who thought she was the Virgin Mary had always been talking about her son. He thought Ignacio looked a little like Jesus. He tried to remember if his mother had ever told him stories when he was at home, and decided that she had not; she just turned on the comscreen to the cartoons.

"—wanted to—"

"—tell a story," Nicholas finished for him.

"How did you know?" Angry and surprised.

"It was you, wasn't it? And you want to tell one now."

"What you said was not what Ignacio would have said. He was going to tell you about a fish."

"Where is it?" Nicholas asked, thinking of the fish Ignacio had been eating the night before, and imagining another such fish, caught while he had been coming back, perhaps, from the Point, and now concealed somewhere waiting the fire. "Is it a big one?"

"It is gone now," Ignacio said, "but it was only as long as a man's hand. I caught it in the big river."

Huckleberry—"I know, the Mississippi; it was a catfish. Or a sunfish."—*Finn.*

"Possibly that is what you call them; for a time he was as the sun to a certain one." The light from nowhere danced on the water. "In any event he was kept on that table in the salon in the house where life was lived. In a tank, but not the old kind in which one sees the glass, with metal at the corner. But the new kind in which the glass is so strong, but very thin, and curved so that it does not reflect, and there are no corners, and a clever device holds the water clear." He dipped up a handful of sparkling water, still not meeting Nicholas's eyes. "As clear even as this, and there were no ripples, and so you could not see it at all. My fish floated in the center of my table above a few stones."

Nicholas asked, "Did you float on the river on a raft?"

"No, we had a little boat. Ignacio caught this fish in a net, of which he almost bit through the strands before he could be landed; he possessed wonderful teeth. There was no one in the house but him and the other, and the robots; but each morning someone would go to the pool in the patio and catch a goldfish for him. Ignacio would see this goldfish there when he came down for his breakfast, and would think, 'Brave goldfish, you have been cast to the monster, will you be the one to destroy him? Destroy him and you shall have his diamond house forever.' And then the fish, who had a little spot of red beneath his wonderful teeth, a spot like a cherry, would rush upon that young goldfish, and for an instant the water would be all clouded with blood."

"And then what?" Nicholas asked.

"And then the clever machine would make the water clear once more, and the fish would be floating above the stones as before, the fish with the wonderful teeth, and Ignacio would touch the little switch on the table, and ask for more bread, and more fruit."

"Are you hungry now?"

"No, I am tired and lazy now; if I pursue you I will not catch you, and if I catch you—through your own slowness and clumsiness—I will not kill you, and if I kill you I will not eat you."

Nicholas had begun to back away, and at the last words, realizing that they were a signal, he turned and began to run, splashing through the shallow water. Ignacio ran after him, much helped by his longer legs, his hair flying behind his dark young face, his square teeth—each white as a bone and as big as Nicholas' thumbnail—showing like spectators who lined the railings of his lips.

"Don't run, Nicholas," Dr. Island said with the voice of a wave. "It only makes him angry that you run." Nicholas did not answer, but cut to his left, up the beach and among the trunks of the palms, sprinting all the way because he had no way of knowing Ignacio was not right behind him, about to grab him by the neck. When he stopped it was in the thick jungle, among the boles of the hardwoods, where he leaned, out of breath, the thumping of his own heart the only sound in an atmosphere silent and unwaked as Earth's long, prehuman day. For a time he listened for any sound Ignacio might make searching for him; there was none. He drew a deep breath then and said, "Well, that's over," expecting Dr. Island to answer from somewhere; there was only the green hush.

The light was still bright and strong and nearly shadowless, but some interior sense told him the day was nearly over, and he noticed that such faint shades as he could see stretched long, horizontal distortions of their objects. He felt no hunger, but he had fasted before and knew on which side of hunger he stood; he was not as strong as he had been only a day past, and by this time next day he would probably be unable to outrun Ignacio. He should, he now realized, have eaten the monkey he had killed; but his stomach revolted at the thought of the raw flesh, and he did not know how he might build a fire, although Ignacio seemed to have done so the night before. Raw fish, even if he were able to catch a fish, would be as bad, or worse, than raw monkey; he remembered his effort to open a coconut—he had failed, but it was surely not impossible. His mind was hazy as to what a coconut might contain, but there had to be an edible core, because they were eaten in books. He decided to make a wide sweep through the jungle that would bring him back to the beach well away from Ignacio; he had several times seen coconuts lying in the sand under the trees.

He moved quietly, still a little afraid, trying to think of ways to open the coconut when he found it. He imagined himself standing before a large and raggedly faceted stone, holding the coconut in both hands. He raised it and smashed it down, but when it struck it was no longer a coconut but Maya's head; he heard her nose cartilage break with a distinct, rubbery snap. Her eyes, as blue as the sky above Madhya Pradesh, the sparkling blue sky of the egg, looked up at him, but he could no longer look into them, they retreated from his own, and it came to him quite suddenly that Lucifer, in falling, must have fallen up, into the fires and the coldness of space, never again to see the warm blues and browns and greens of Earth: *I was watching Satan fall as lightning from heaven.* He had heard that on tape somewhere, but he could not remember where. He had read that on Earth lightning did not come down from the clouds, but leaped up from the planetary surface toward them, never to return.

"Nicholas."

He listened, but did not hear his name again. Faintly water was babbling; had Dr. Island used that sound to speak to him? He walked toward it and found a little rill that threaded a way among the trees, and followed it. In a hundred steps it grew broader, slowed, and ended in a long blind pool under a dome of leaves. Diane was sitting on moss on the side opposite him; she looked up as she saw him, and smiled.

"Hello," he said.

"Hello, Nicholas. I thought I heard you. I wasn't mistaken after all, was I?"

"I didn't think I said anything." He tested the dark water with his foot and found that it was very cold.

"You gave a little gasp, I fancy. I heard it, and I said to myself, *that's Nicholas,* and I called you. Then I thought I might be wrong, or that it might be Ignacio."

"Ignacio was chasing me. Maybe he still is, but I think he's probably given up by now."

The girl nodded, looking into the dark waters of the pool, but did not seem to have heard him. He began to work his way around to her, climbing across the snakelike roots of the crowding trees. "Why does Ignacio want to kill me, Diane?"

"Sometimes he wants to kill me too," the girl said.

"But why?"

"I think he's a bit frightened of us. Have you ever talked to him, Nicholas?"

"Today I did a little. He told me a story about a pet fish he used to have."

"Ignacio grew up all alone; did he tell you that? On Earth. On a plantation in Brazil, way up the Amazon—Dr. Island told me."

"I thought it was crowded on Earth."

"The cities are crowded, and the countryside closest to the cities. But there are places where it's emptier than it used to be. Where Ignacio was, there would have been Red Indian hunters two or three hundred years ago; when he was there, there wasn't anyone, just the machines. Now he doesn't want to be looked at, doesn't want anyone around him."

Nicholas said slowly, "Dr. Island said lots of people wouldn't be sick if only there weren't other people around all the time. Remember that?"

"Only there are other people around all the time; that's how the world is."

"Not in Brazil, maybe," Nicholas said. He was trying to remember something about Brazil, but the only thing he could think of was a parrot singing in a straw hat from the comview cartoons; and then a turtle and a hedgehog that turned into armadillos for the love of God, Montressor. He said, "Why didn't he stay there?"

"Did I tell you about the bird, Nicholas?" She had been not-listening again.

"What bird?"

"I have a bird. Inside." She patted the flat stomach below her small breasts, and for a moment Nicholas thought she had really found food. "She sits in here. She has tangled a nest in my entrails, where she sits and tears at my breath with her beak. I look healthy to you, don't I? But inside I'm hollow and rotten and turning brown, dirt and old feathers, oozing away. Her beak will break through soon."

"Okay." Nicholas turned to go.

"I've been drinking water here, trying to drown her. I think I've swallowed so much I couldn't stand up now if I tried, but she isn't even wet, and do you know something, Nicholas? I've found out I'm not really me, I'm her."

Turning back Nicholas asked, "When was the last time you had anything to eat?"

"I don't know. Two, three days ago. Ignacio gave me something."

"I'm going to try to open a coconut. If I can I'll bring you back some."

When he reached the beach, Nicholas turned and walked slowly back in the direction of the dead fire, this time along the rim of dampened sand between the sea and the palms. He was thinking about machines.

There were hundreds of thousands, perhaps millions, of machines out beyond the belt, but few or none of the sophisticated servant robots of Earth—those were luxuries. Would Ignacio, in Brazil (whatever that was like), have had such luxuries? Nicholas thought not; those robots were almost like people, and living with them would be like living with people. Nicholas wished that he could speak Brazilian.

There had been the therapy robots at St. John's; Nicholas had not liked them, and he did not think Ignacio would have liked them either. If he had liked his therapy robot he probably would not have had to be sent here. He thought of the chipped and rusted old machine that had cleaned the corridors—Maya had called it Corradora, but no one else ever called it anything but *Hey!* It could not (or at least did not) speak, and Nicholas doubted that it had emotions, except possibly a sort of love of cleanness that did not extend to its own person. "You will understand," someone was saying inside his head, "that motives of all sorts can be divided into two sorts." A doctor? A therapy robot? It did not matter. "Extrinsic and intrinsic. An extrinsic motive has always some further end in view, and that end we call an intrinsic motive. Thus when we have reduced motivation to intrinsic motivation we have reduced it to its simplest parts. Take that machine over there."

What machine?

"Freud would have said that it was fixated at the latter anal stage, perhaps due to the care its builders exercised in seeing that the dirt it collects is not released again. Because of its fixation it is, as you see, obsessed with cleanliness and order; compulsive sweeping and scrubbing palliate its anxieties. It is a strength of Freud's theory, and not a weakness, that it serves to explain many of the activities of machines as well as the acts of persons."

Hello there, Corradora.

And hello, Ignacio.

My head, moving from side to side, must remind you of a radar scanner. My steps are measured, slow, and precise. I emit a scarcely audible humming as I walk, and my eyes are fixed, as I swing my head, not on you, Ignacio, but on the waves at the edge of sight, where they curve up into the sky. I stop ten meters short of you, and I stand.

You go, I follow, ten meters behind. What do I want? Nothing.

Yes, I will pick up the sticks, and I will follow—five meters behind.

"Break them, and put them on the fire. Not all of them, just a few."

Yes.

"Ignacio keeps the fire here burning all the time. Sometimes he takes the coals of fire from it to start others, but here, under the big palm log, he has a fire always. The rain does not strike it here. Always the fire. Do you know how he made it the first time? Reply to him!"

"No."

"No, *Patrão!*"

" 'No, *Patrão.*' "

"Ignacio stole it from the gods, from Poseidon. Now Poseidon is dead, lying at the bottom of the water. Which is the top. Would you like to see him?"

"If you wish it, *Patrão.*"

"It will soon be dark, and that is the time to fish; do you have a spear?"

"No, *Patrão.*"

"Then Ignacio will get you one."

Ignacio took a handful of the sticks and thrust the ends into the fire, blowing on them. After a moment Nicholas leaned over and blew too, until all the sticks were blazing.

"Now we must find you some bamboo, and there is some back here. Follow me."

The light, still nearly shadowless, was dimming now, so that it seemed to Nicholas that they walked on insubstantial soil, though he could feel it beneath his feet. Ignacio stalked ahead, holding up the burning sticks until the fire seemed about to die, then pointing the ends down, allowing it to lick upward toward his hand and come to life again. There was a gentle wind blowing out toward the sea, carrying away the sound of the surf and bringing a damp coolness; and when they had been walking for several minutes, Nicholas heard in it a faint, dry, almost rhythmic rattle.

Ignacio looked back at him and said, "The music. The big stems talking; hear it?"

They found a cane a little thinner than Nicholas's wrist and piled the burning sticks around its base, then added more. When it fell, Ignacio burned through the upper end too, making a pole about as long as Nicholas was tall, and with the edge of a seashell scraped the larger end to a point. "Now you are a fisherman," he said. Nicholas said, "Yes, *Patrão,*" still careful not to meet his eyes.

"You are hungry?"

"Yes, *Patrão.*"

"Then let me tell you something. Whatever you get is Ignacio's, you understand? And what he catches, that is his too. But when he has eaten what he wants, what is left is yours. Come on now, and Ignacio will teach you to fish or drown you."

Ignacio's own spear was buried in the sand not far from the fire; it was much bigger than the one he had made for Nicholas. With it held across his chest he went down to the water, wading until it was waist high, then swimming, not looking to see if Nicholas was following. Nicholas found that he could swim with the spear by putting all his effort into the motion of his legs, holding the spear in his left hand and stroking only occasionally with his right. "You breathe," he said softly, "and watch the spear," and after that he had only to allow his head to lift from time to time.

He had thought Ignacio would begin to look for fish as soon as they were well out from the beach, but the Brazilian continued to swim, slowly but steadily, until it seemed to Nicholas that they must be a kilometer or more from land. Suddenly, as though the lights in a room had responded to a switch, the dark sea around them became an opalescent blue. Ignacio stopped, treading water and using his spear to buoy himself.

"Here," he said. "Get them between yourself and the light."

Open-eyed, he bent his face to the water, raised it again to breathe deeply, and dove. Nicholas followed his example, floating belly-down with open eyes.

All the world of dancing glitter and dark island vanished as though he had plunged his face into a dream. Far, far below him Jupiter displayed its broad, striped disk, marred with the spreading Bright Spot where man-made silicone enzymes had stripped the hydrogen from methane for kindled fusion: a cancer and a burning infant sun. Between that sun and his eyes lay invisible a hundred thousand kilometers of space, and the temperglass shell of the satellite; hundreds of meters of illuminated water, and in it the spread body of Ignacio, dark against the light, still kicking downward, his spear a pencil line of blackness in his hand.

Involuntarily Nicholas' head came up, returning to the

universe of sparkling waves, aware now that what he had called "night" was only the shadow cast by Dr. Island when Jupiter and the Bright Spot slid beneath her. That shadow line, indetectable in air, now lay sharp across the water behind him. He took breath and plunged.

Almost at once a fish darted somewhere below, and his left arm thrust the spear forward, but it was far out of reach. He swam after it, then saw another, larger, fish farther down and dove for that, passing Ignacio surfacing for air. The fish was too deep, and he had used up his oxygen; his lungs aching for air, he swam up, wanting to let go of his spear, then realizing at the last moment that he could, that it would only bob to the surface if he released it. His head broke water and he gasped, his heart thumping; water struck his face and he knew again, suddenly, as though they had ceased to exist while he was gone, the pulsebeat pounding of the waves.

Ignacio was waiting for him. He shouted, "This time you will come with Ignacio, and he will show you the dead sea god. Then we will fish."

Unable to speak, Nicholas nodded. He was allowed three more breaths; then Ignacio dove and Nicholas had to follow, kicking down until the pressure sang in his ears. Then through blue water he saw, looming at the edge of the light, a huge mass of metal anchored to the temperglass hull of the satellite itself; above it, hanging lifelessly like the stem of a great vine severed from the root, a cable twice as thick as a man's body; and on the bottom, sprawled beside the mighty anchor, a legged god that might have been a dead insect save that it was at least six meters long. Ignacio turned and looked back at Nicholas to see if he understood; he did not, but he nodded, and with the strength draining from his arms, surfaced again.

After Ignacio brought up the first fish, they took turns on the surface guarding their catch, and while the Bright Spot crept beneath the shelving rim of Dr. Island, they speared

two more, one of them quite large. Then when Nicholas was
so exhausted he could scarcely lift his arms, they made their
way back to shore, and Ignacio showed him how to gut the
fish with a thorn and the edge of a shell, and reclose them and
pack them in mud and leaves to be roasted by the fire. After
Ignacio had begun to eat the largest fish, Nicholas timidly
drew out the smallest, and ate for the first time since coming
to Dr. Island. Only when he had finished did he remember
Diane.

He did not dare to take the last fish to her, but he looked
covertly at Ignacio, and began edging away from the fire.
The Brazilian seemed not to have noticed him. When he was
well into the shadows he stood, backed a few steps, then—
slowly, as his instincts warned him—walked away, not beginning to trot until the distance between them was nearly a
hundred meters.

He found Diane sitting apathetic and silent at the margin
of the cold pool, and had some difficulty persuading her to
stand. At last he lifted her, his hands under her arms pressing
against her thin ribs. Once on her feet she stood steadily
enough, and followed him when he took her by the hand. He
talked to her, knowing that although she gave no sign of
hearing she heard him, and that the right words might wake
her to response. "We went fishing—Ignacio showed me how.
And he's got a fire, Diane, he got it from a kind of robot that
was supposed to be fixing one of the cables that holds Dr.
Island, I don't know how. Anyway, listen, we caught three
big fish, and I ate one and Ignacio ate a great big one, and
I don't think he'd mind if you had the other one, only say,
'Yes, *Patrão,*' and 'No, *Patrão,*' to him—he likes that, and he's
only used to machines. You don't have to smile at him or
anything—just look at the fire, that's what I do, just look at
the fire."

To Ignacio, perhaps wisely, he at first said nothing at all,
leading Diane to the place where he had been sitting himself
a few minutes before and placing some scraps from his fish

in her lap. When she did not eat he found a sliver of the tender, roasted flesh and thrust it into her mouth. Ignacio said, "Ignacio believed that one dead," and Nicholas answered, "No, *Patrão.*"

"There is another fish. Give it to her."

Nicholas did, raking the gob of baked mud from the coals to crack with the heel of his hand, and peeling the broken and steaming fillets from the skin and bones to give to her when they had cooled enough to eat; after the fish had lain in her mouth for perhaps half a minute she began to chew and swallow, and after the third mouthful she fed herself, though without looking at either of them.

"Ignacio believed that one dead," Ignacio said again.

"No, *Patrão,*" Nicholas answered, and then added, "Like you can see, she's alive."

"She is a pretty creature, with the firelight on her face—no?"

"Yes, *Patrão,* very pretty."

"But too thin." Ignacio moved around the fire until he was sitting almost beside Diane, then reached for the fish Nicholas had given her. Her hands closed on it, though she still did not look at him.

"You see, she knows us after all," Ignacio said. "We are not ghosts."

Nicholas whispered urgently, "Let him have it."

Slowly Diane's fingers relaxed, but Ignacio did not take the fish. "I was only joking, little one," he said. "And I think not such a good joke after all." Then when she did not reply, he turned away from her, his eyes reaching out across the dark, tossing water for something Nicholas could not see.

"She likes you, *Patrão,*" Nicholas said. The words were like swallowing filth, but he thought of the bird ready to tear through Diane's skin, and Maya's blood soaking in little round dots into the white cloth, and continued. "She is only shy. It is better that way."

"You. What do you know?"

At least Ignacio was no longer looking at the sea. Nicholas said, "Isn't it true, *Patrão?*"

"Yes, it is true."

Diane was picking at the fish again, conveying tiny flakes to her mouth with delicate fingers; distinctly but almost absently she said, "Go, Nicholas."

He looked at Ignacio, but the Brazilian's eyes did not turn toward the girl, nor did he speak.

"Nicholas, go away. Please."

In a voice he hoped was pitched too low for Ignacio to hear, Nicholas said, "I'll see you in the morning. All right?"

Her head moved a fraction of a centimeter.

Once he was out of sight of the fire, one part of the beach was as good to sleep on as another; he wished he had taken a piece of wood from the fire to start one of his own and tried to cover his legs with sand to keep off the cool wind, but the sand fell away whenever he moved, and his legs and his left hand moved without volition on his part.

The surf, lapping at the rippled shore, said, "That was well done, Nicholas."

"I can feel you move," Nicholas said. "I don't think I ever could before except when I was high up."

"I doubt that you can now; my roll is less than one one-hundredth of a degree."

"Yes, I can. You wanted me to do that, didn't you? About Ignacio."

"Do you know what the Harlow effect is, Nicholas?"

Nicholas shook his head.

"About a hundred years ago Dr. Harlow experimented with monkeys who had been raised in complete isolation— no mothers, no other monkeys at all."

"Lucky monkeys."

"When the monkeys were mature he put them into cages with normal ones; they fought with any that came near them, and sometimes they killed them."

"Psychologists always put things in cages; did he ever think of turning them loose in the jungle instead?"

"No, Nicholas, though we have . . . Aren't you going to say anything?"

"I guess not."

"Dr. Harlow tried, you see, to get the isolate monkeys to breed—sex is the primary social function—but they wouldn't. Whenever another monkey of either sex approached they displayed aggressiveness, which the other monkeys returned. He cured them finally by introducing immature monkeys—monkey children—in place of the mature, socialized ones. These needed the isolate adults so badly that they kept on making approaches no matter how often or how violently they were rejected, and in the end they were accepted, and the isolates socialized. It's interesting to note that the founder of Christianity seems to have had an intuitive grasp of the principle—but it was almost two thousand years before it was demonstrated scientifically."

"I don't think it worked here," Nicholas said. "It was more complicated than that."

"Human beings are complicated monkeys, Nicholas."

"That's about the first time I ever heard you make a joke. You like not being human, don't you?"

"Of course. Wouldn't you?"

"I always thought I would, but now I'm not sure. You said that to help me, didn't you? I don't like that."

A wave higher than the others splashed chill foam over Nicholas's legs, and for a moment he wondered if this were Dr. Island's reply. Half a minute later another wave wet him, and another, and he moved farther up the beach to avoid them. The wind was stronger, but he slept despite it, and was awakened only for a moment by a flash of light from the direction from which he had come; he tried to guess what might have caused it, thought of Diane and Ignacio throwing the burning sticks into the air to see the arcs of fire, smiled —too sleepy now to be angry—and slept again.

Morning came cold and sullen; Nicholas ran up and down the beach, rubbing himself with his hands. A thin rain, or spume (it was hard to tell which), was blowing in the wind, clouding the light to gray radiance. He wondered if Diane and Ignacio would mind if he came back now and decided to wait, then thought of fishing so that he would have something to bring when he came; but the sea was very cold and the waves so high they tumbled him, wrenching his bamboo spear from his hand. Ignacio found him dripping with water, sitting with his back to a palm trunk and staring out toward the lifting curve of the sea.

"Hello, you," Ignacio said.

"Good morning, *Patrão.*"

Ignacio sat down. "What is your name? You told me, I think, when we first met, but I have forgotten. I am sorry."

"Nicholas."

"Yes."

"Patrão, I am very cold. Would it be possible for us to go to your fire?"

"My name is Ignacio; call me that."

Nicholas nodded, frightened.

"But we cannot go to my fire, because the fire is out."

"Can't you make another one, *Patrão?*"

"You do not trust me, do you? I do not blame you. No, I cannot make another—you may use what I had, if you wish, and make one after I have gone. I came only to say goodbye."

"You're leaving?"

The wind in the palm fronds said, "Ignacio is much better now. He will be going to another place, Nicholas."

"A hospital?"

"Yes, a hospital, but I don't think he will have to stay there long."

"But . . ." Nicholas tried to think of something appropriate. At St. John's and the other places where he had been confined, when people left, they simply left, and usually were hardly spoken of once it was learned that they were going and thus were already tainted by whatever it was that froze the smiles and dried the tears of those outside. At last he said, "Thanks for teaching me how to fish."

"That was all right," Ignacio said. He stood up and put a hand on Nicholas's shoulder, then turned away. Four meters to his left the damp sand was beginning to lift and crack. While Nicholas watched, it opened on a brightly lit companionway walled with white. Ignacio pushed his curly black hair back from his eyes and went down, and the sand closed with a thump.

"He won't be coming back, will he?" Nicholas said.

"No."

"He said I could use his stuff to start another fire, but I don't even know what it is."

Dr. Island did not answer. Nicholas got up and began to walk back to where the fire had been, thinking about Diane and wondering if she was hungry; he was hungry himself.

He found her beside the dead fire. Her chest had been burned away, and lying close by, near the hole in the sand where Ignacio must have kept it hidden, was a bulky nuclear welder. The power pack was too heavy for Nicholas to lift, but he picked up the welding gun on its short cord and touched the trigger, producing a two-meter plasma discharge which he played along the sand until Diane's body was ash. By the time he had finished the wind was whipping the palms and sending stinging rain into his eyes, but he collected a supply of wood and built another fire, bigger and bigger until it roared like a forge in the wind. "He killed her!" he shouted to the waves.

"YES." Dr. Island's voice was big and wild.

"You said he was better."

"HE IS," howled the wind. "YOU KILLED THE MONKEY THAT WANTED TO PLAY WITH YOU, NICHOLAS—AS I BE-

LIEVED IGNACIO WOULD EVENTUALLY KILL YOU, WHO ARE
SO EASILY HATED, SO DIFFERENT FROM WHAT IT IS THOUGHT
A BOY SHOULD BE. BUT KILLING THE MONKEY HELPED YOU,
REMEMBER? MADE YOU BETTER. IGNACIO WAS FRIGHTENED
BY WOMEN; NOW HE KNOWS THAT THEY ARE REALLY VERY
WEAK, AND HE HAS ACTED UPON CERTAIN FANTASIES AND
FINDS THEM BITTER."

"You're rocking," Nicholas said. "Am I doing that?"

"YOUR THOUGHT."

A palm snapped in the storm; instead of falling, it flew
crashing among the others, its fronded head catching the
wind like a sail. "I'm killing you," Nicholas said. "Destroying
you." The left side of his face was so contorted with grief and
rage that he could scarcely speak.

Dr. Island heaved beneath his feet. "NO."

"One of your cables is already broken—I saw that. Maybe
more than one. You'll pull loose. I'm turning this world, isn't
that right? The attitude rockets are tuned to my emotions,
and they're spinning us around, and the slippage is the wind
and the high sea, and when you come loose nothing will
balance any more."

"NO."

"What's the stress on your cables? Don't you know?"

"THEY ARE VERY STRONG."

"What kind of talk is that? You ought to say something like:
'The D-twelve cable tension is twenty-billion kilograms'
force. WARNING! WARNING! Expected time to failure is nine-
ty-seven seconds! WARNING!' *Don't you even know how a
machine is supposed to talk?*" Nicholas was screaming now,
and every wave reached farther up the beach than the last,
so that the bases of the most seaward palms were awash.

"GET BACK, NICHOLAS. FIND HIGHER GROUND. GO INTO
THE JUNGLE." It was the crashing waves themselves that
spoke.

"I won't."

A long serpent of water reached for the fire, which hissed and sputtered.

"GET BACK!"

"I won't!"

A second wave came, striking Nicholas calf-high and nearly extinguishing the fire.

"ALL THIS WILL BE UNDER WATER SOON. GET BACK!"

Nicholas picked up some of the still-burning sticks and tried to carry them, but the wind blew them out as soon as he lifted them from the fire. He tugged at the welder, but it was too heavy for him to lift.

"GET BACK!"

He went into the jungle, where the trees lashed themselves to leafy rubbish in the wind and broken branches flew through the air like debris from an explosion; for a while he heard Diane's voice crying in the wind; it became Maya's, then his mother's or Sister Carmela's, and a hundred others; in time the wind grew less, and he could no longer feel the ground rocking. He felt tired. He said, "I didn't kill you after all, did I?" but there was no answer. On the beach, when he returned to it, he found the welder half buried in sand. No trace of Diane's ashes, nor of his fire. He gathered more wood and built another, lighting it with the welder.

"Now," he said. He scooped aside the sand around the welder until he reached the rough understone beneath it, and turned the flame of the welder on that; it blackened and bubbled.

"No," Dr. Island said.

"Yes." He was bending intently over the flame, both hands locked on the welder's trigger.

"Nicholas, stop that." When he did not reply, "Look behind you." There was a splashing louder than the crashing of the waves, and a groaning of metal. He whirled and saw the great, beetle-like robot Ignacio had shown him on the sea floor. Tiny shellfish clung to its metal skin, and water, faintly green, still poured from its body. Before he could turn the welding gun toward it, it shot forward hands like clamps and wrenched it from him. All up and down the beach similar machines were smoothing the sand and repairing the damage of the storm.

"That thing was dead," Nicholas said. "Ignacio killed it."

It picked up the power pack, shook it clean of sand, and turning, stalked back toward the sea.

"That is what Ignacio believed, and it was better that he believed so."

"And you said you couldn't do anything, you had no hands."

"I also told you that I would treat you as society will when you are released, that that was my nature. After that, did you still believe all I told you? Nicholas, you are upset now because Diane is dead—"

"You could have protected her!"

"—but by dying she made someone else—someone very important—well. Her prognosis was bad; she really wanted only death, and this was the death I chose for her. You could call it the death of Dr. Island, a death that would help someone else. Now you are alone, but soon there will be more patients in this segment, and you will help them, too—if you can—and perhaps they will help you. Do you understand?"

"No," Nicholas said. He flung himself down on the sand. The wind had dropped, but it was raining hard. He thought of the vision he had once had, and of describing it to Diane the day before. "This isn't ending the way I thought," he whispered. It was only a squeak of sound far down in his throat. "Nothing ever turns out right."

The waves, the wind, the rustling palm fronds and the pattering rain, the monkeys who had come down to the beach to search for food washed ashore, answered, "Go away —go back—don't move."

Nicholas pressed his scarred head against his knees, rocking back and forth.

"Don't move."

For a long time he sat still while the rain lashed his shoulders and the dripping monkeys frolicked and fought around him. When at last he lifted his face, there was in it some element of personality which had been only potentially present before, and with this an emptiness and an expression of surprise. His lips moved, and the sounds were the sounds made by a deaf-mute who tries to speak.

"Nicholas is gone," the waves said. "Nicholas, who was the right side of your body, the left half of your brain, I have forced into catatonia; for the remainder of your life he will be to you only what you once were to him—or less. Do you understand?"

The boy nodded.

"We will call you Kenneth, silent one. And if Nicholas tries to come again, Kenneth, you must drive him back—or return to what you have been."

The boy nodded a second time, and a moment afterward began to collect sticks for the dying fire. As though to themselves the waves chanted:

> "Seas are wild tonight . . .
> Stretching over Sado island
> Silent clouds of stars."

There was no reply.

THE GHOST WRITER

by Geo. Alec Effinger

Geo. Alec Effinger was nominated for a Hugo Award for "All the Last Wars At Once," his story in Universe 1; *the final balloting is taking place as this book goes to press, but win or lose, Effinger is obviously beginning to make his mark in science fiction. Here he writes a tale of our distant future, when art is no longer as we know it . . . but artists may not have changed so much. (Maybe one of those faraway writers will someday rediscover this very story; if so, I wonder what they might think of it . . .)*

Effinger's first novel, What Entropy Means to Me, *was published in 1972.*

HE WAS performing before several hundred million people, although he himself was the only person in the huge stadium. Concentric circles of transparent plastic slabs surrounded him, beginning only a few yards from his feet at the edge of the low stage and rising higher and higher, until the farthest row of seats was lost in the late evening's darkness. Each of the places was occupied by a wandering consciousness, directed and guarded out-of-body by TECT.

Anabben did not put on as energetic a show as the greater writers, but his stories themselves had a greater vigor. Although many of the audience had come to hear Phioth, the majority had been drawn also by the hope of hearing a long and exciting fragment from Anabben.

He sat in a chair in the middle of the shiny black stage. His feet were on the floor, close together, and his hands were resting in his lap. His head did not droop forward, but his expression was drugged and sleepy. Phioth would not sit; no, the greatest of the writers would dash about his small area, shouting his story, or whispering, and earning his fame as much with his acting as with his words.

This fragment was a particularly long one for Anabben. On the three previous exhibitions his story had ended within thirty minutes; the fragments had seemed unrelated, and none had even come close to being complete. There was always the chance that a new fragment might join two of the enigmatic earlier pieces, and a whole framework might begin to be evident. But not today. Here was another piece, of perhaps a totally different puzzle. It was longer, and it was exciting. The audience would be satisfied, but not the scholars.

"He threw another bomb," said Anabben, reciting slowly with only a minimum of inflection. *"A department store fell*

*in upon itself. Shards of brick and glass rained about him,
and he was cut and bleeding. He felt nothing but a weird
elation. The sound of authority in the explosion, the sound
of tons of concrete and steel falling, the sound of hundreds
of windows shattering—all these were strangely comforting
and exciting to him."*

Many words were unintelligible to those who listened, and
indeed, the basic conflict of the story was meaningless. In
some way a man seemed to be acting *differently,* in a new
manner unlike people. In many of the stories told by the
writers, people behaved in frightening patterns. A small
number of persons had stopped attending the performances,
protesting that the stories might teach one to act so *differently.* It would be the scholars, with the creative resources
of TECT, who would ponder the meaning of the strange
words: *bomb, authority, concrete.*

Anabben continued. *"In the middle of the twisted and
charred rubble knelt."* He fell silent. It was clear that he had
ended in the middle of a sentence. The audience, in their
millions of scattered homes, sighed. Anabben sat quietly for
a few moments. Gradually his face became more animated
as he appeared to awaken from a deep trance. He stood,
alone in the immense stadium, and walked to the edge of the
stage. He was tired.

Anabben sat down, awaiting the next performance. He was
alone; Vakeis was in his house. Her empty body rested on the
low couch by the pond. Anabben guessed that her mind was
still here at the stadium, waiting for the great Phioth. Anabben smiled ruefully. How could he expect Vakeis to be waiting for him, when Phioth was performing? He indulged himself in a little jealousy, an emotion rare for people but just
eccentric enough for writers. As a writer he had a permanent
slab reserved at the stadium. He knew that thousands of
people unable to attend the performance would be horrified
at his lack of interest.

He decided to stay because Phioth *did* entertain. And, since he was the greatest of them all, each performance held an element of history. TECT had lit the stage, for the sky was black, now. Phioth appeared from the tect near where Anabben was sitting. Anabben watched him go to the chair in the center of the stage. Phioth's hands grasped the arms of the chair, and one thumb found the small groove where a small amount of relaxant would prepare him for the exhibition. Unless Phioth's mind was calm and unafraid, it would not find its goal when TECT hurled it into the great death stream.

Every year TECT was used to send the consciousnesses of dozens of aspiring writers, each hoping to align itself with the drifting residue of an ancient master. Sometimes, as with Phioth, there was good fortune, and the young man's self would find a comfortable mate. Most often, however, there were no minds waiting to meet the adventurer, and instead of glory, there was raving panic. Of course TECT *made* each of these unfortunates *away*, and only the other writers had seen the terrifying display of a living man with his mind in death.

Phioth approached the chair with confidence, though, having made the journey many times and knowing that a welcoming soul waited for him. There were countless elder intellects abandoned to the strange flaming plane after their bodies died. But if the youthful volunteer did not have a mind suitably attuned to one of them, the ghostly traffic was of no use. If the writer were lucky, he would return sane, with a small scrap of lost literature. If the man were supremely lucky, he would find himself matched with a legendary genius, a reflection of his own innate powers.

Phioth was the luckiest, and the greatest, of all the writers. After two centuries of fishing the mind stream, one man had become William Shakespeare/Phioth. Although none of Shakespeare's works remained in the world, as no literature of any sort existed, the Elizabethan's reputation had lived and grown. Phioth's audiences listened excitedly, for every new fragment that he brought back was heard on earth for the first time in two thousand years.

"Resembles what it was," said Phioth, still in the chair. He rose slowly and, while his face kept the possessed look of the performing writer, his body paced the narrow stage. His hands flew about, pointing, gesturing, threatening. His voice shifted in both tone and tempo, and Anabben marveled at the impact of the nearly senseless words.

> *"What it should be,*
> *More than his father's death, that thus hath put him*
> *So much from the understanding of himself,*
> *I cannot dream of. I entreat you both,*
> *That, being of so young days brought up with him*
> *And since so neighbour'd to his youth and humour,*
> *That you vouchsafe your rest here in our court*
> *Some little time; so by your companies . . ."*

Anabben watched enviously. Phioth marched back and forth across the scanty thumbnail stage, and Anabben was caught up in the flurry of motion. This sort of behavior was so provocative, so *different,* that Anabben wondered that the tectmen did not come to *make* Phioth *away.* Here were not only great, dead words, but also some nameless feeling from the past, a dangerous passion that aroused Anabben. The people of Anabben's time had rediscovered the idea of theater, that certain products of the writer's mind were to be more than merely read. The scholars and TECT had made a vague reconstruction of the forms of literature, based on the several sorts of fragments they received from their writers.

Phioth spoke on as Anabben considered his own popularity. It was obvious from the content of the story fragments that his source was of another time than Shakespeare.

Each writer knew the identity of his long-dead tutor, felt it intimately housed within his transported mind until the connection weakened and the tired vessel awoke. Anabben spoke the stories of one Sandor Courane; the scholars knew nothing about him, and they argued his merits relative to Shakespeare. Courane was less subtle, less universal, but more—involving. Courane had greater popular appeal, and such a phenomenon required study. It was not for Anabben to care what the factors were that maintained his distinction. He secretly enjoyed his fame and, even more secretly, wished ill for Phioth.

"—*And I do think,*" said Phioth, his fist clenched above his head, "*or else this brain of mine*

> *Hunts not the trail of policy so sure*
> *As it hath us'd to do, that I have found*
> *The very cause of Hamlet's lunacy.*"

Hamlet! Another piece of that famous myth. The scholars must be squealing now, thought Anabben. On an impulse he got up, stepped into the tect, and transported home.

The grass was cool beneath his feet. Among the random pieces of roof Anabben could see the first quiet flush of stars. Thin, widely separated panels stood here and there to support the patches of roof and the house's mechanisms. Among them trees grew, brooks ran, and furniture stood ready for service. At the bottom of the hill Anabben saw a dim light around the couch where Vakeis' body still rested, while she observed Phioth's grandiose performance.

The air was chill, and Anabben requested TECT to raise the temperature of his outdoor home. As an afterthought he had the entire area of his estate lit brightly. TECT scattered the night, broke the darkness into ragged shadows, and chased even these small bits of shade among the roots of the trees. Anabben felt better. He walked down to the pond and sat down in the grass opposite his mistress. He waited for Phioth to end.

In a few minutes Vakeis stirred. She sat up and rubbed her neck, which had become stiff during the long period while her mind traveled to the stadium. She noticed Anabben and smiled. "You're back early," she said, with a puzzled expression.

"I was very tired," said Anabben. He did not return her smile. "I saw only a little of Phioth's reading. *Hamlet* again, wasn't it?"

"Yes. Very beautiful, but strange. I'm sorry you didn't stay. There must be thousands who would have given their Vote to see him."

"I know," said Anabben, standing and holding out his hand to her. They walked around the pond, which, through TECT, Anabben kept frozen all year long. He led her back up the hill to the meeting area. He did not feel like talking, knowing that anything that he said would lead her to a discussion of Phioth.

"I enjoyed your performance, dear," she said.

"I'm glad. Of course, I can't remember it. Maybe if Charait and the others come over tonight I'll play it. It is sad how my own work interests me so little."

"I don't believe you," said Vakeis, picking a clump of grass and tossing it toward Anabben's head. He ducked, and it missed him. He did not laugh.

"No, really," he said. "I don't even know why I bother. When you're competing with someone like Phioth, it's hard to take yourself seriously."

"Phioth is one thing, you're another." Vakeis could see that Anabben was depressed, more than merely tired from his performance. She tugged at his arm and he stopped walking and looked at her. "Listen," she said, "you know there are just as many people who love your readings."

"Not quite," he said bitterly.

"Well, almost. Shakespeare is a myth. Almost a god. Naturally, people are going to listen to Phioth with different ears. But they *enjoy* your readings more. The two of you aren't even rivals. You appeal to different needs, and you both satisfy those needs equally. You were really wonderful to-night."

"Come on. I suppose they'll be here soon."

Reacting to his boredom and his jealousy, Anabben had TECT kill the lights in the house, leaving only a soft glow on the hill as they walked. He requested faint music, but in his growing impatience he stopped that immediately, too. When they got to the top of the hill, Anabben's meeting area, they saw two men appear from the small tect. The first to arrive was tall and gaunt, with hair braided down to his waist. He wore a pale-blue cloth twined about his body. The second man was shorter and heavier, with closely cut hair and a small beard. He wore no clothing. The new arrivals waved to Anabben and Vakeis, and sat down on the lawn to wait.

"Hello, Charait," said Vakeis, walking up to the man in the blue robe. He touched her leg and kissed her knee, and Vakeis laughed.

"This is Torephes," said Charait, holding up the hand of the other man. "If you can believe it, he wants to perform, too."

Anabben frowned. Charait was no problem; his bits of re-trieved literature were from the works of a Mrs. Lidsake. The scholars, with all the subtle forces of TECT, were unable to place her among the other rediscovered, either qualitatively or chronologically. Charait's performances were interesting from a historical viewpoint, as all performances were, but they were somehow not absorbing. But this new Torephes presented a threat to Anabben, as the potential vessel of another genius that would overshadow Anabben's meager contributions.

"My friend Charait isn't joking," said Anabben. "Only we writers have seen what happens to the unsuccessful aspi-rants. Perhaps if the public knew how awful it is, soon there would be no new writers at all. How much thought have you given to this?"

Torephes looked very uneasy. Anabben made a mental request to TECT, and the temperature in the meeting area was lowered ten degrees.

"It's something that I've *always* wanted," said Torephes. "I understand about the chances. Charait has been warning me for about two years now, but I'm willing." His expression was so determined that Anabben laughed.

"Then let us wait for the others to arrive, and we'll talk about it," said Anabben. "Maybe the inspiration of Phioth has persuaded you unwisely."

Anabben and Vakeis seated themselves next to the two men. Anabben kept silent, and out of embarrassment, Vakeis assumed the role of hostess, asking the guests if they were comfortable, and if they desired refreshment.

"It is a bit cool," said Torephes, still ill-at-ease and fearing to offend such a celebrity as Anabben.

Anabben grunted and had TECT increase the temperature by ten degrees. "The dispenser is in that plane," he said, indicating the single wall in the meeting area. From his comment it was apparent that he was not going to serve his guests, as simple courtesy demanded. Torephes whispered to Charait, and Anabben could hear him suggest that they leave, but Charait just shook his head. After all, Anabben was a writer, the sort of person more inclined to moods than common citizens. And, further, he had just given a performance. Charait took Torephes' arm and led him to the dispenser.

"Vakeis," said Charait, "would you like something?"

"No," she said, "I'll wait."

"Anabben?"

Anabben just frowned and waved. Charait requested a small bowl of meat and flowers, and Torephes had a cup of relaxant and some protein bread.

In a short while three people stepped out of Anabben's tect: a young woman and two old men. They greeted Anabben and his guests, went straight to the dispenser, and joined the others on the grass. The young woman was named Rochei; she was a writer attuned to the poetry of a long-dead person named Elizabeth Dawson Douglas. One of the old men was a famous writer, one whom Anabben envied almost as much as he envied Phioth. His name was Tradenne, and he was also Tertius Publius Ieta. The other man was Briol, who had given his first performance just a few days previously, and had held the audience entranced with a fragment written by Daniel Defoe. Anabben was still sitting sullenly next to Vakeis, and she made the introductions. The easy conversation of the friends stopped when they learned that Torephes wanted to become a writer.

"Did you watch Phioth this evening?" asked Rochei, as she braided Vakeis' long, dark hair.

"Yes," said Torephes. "One of my fathers understands how much I want to perform, and he let me use his place at the stadium."

"Did you enjoy it?" asked Tradenne.

Torephes hesitated. "Phioth is another sort of greatness. You don't *enjoy* him. You *experience* him, if you know what I mean. Not only the genius of Shakespeare, but the genius of Phioth."

"Exactly," said Briol quietly.

"I would be interested to know what you thought of *my* performance," said Anabben.

There was an immediate silence in Anabben's meeting area. Suddenly the atmosphere was tense. It was an unfair question, and even Anabben's notorious peculiarities did not excuse it.

"I thought you were very good," said Torephes after a long pause. "I've enjoyed all of your performances that I've heard through TECT. You're a contrast. Courane is distinctive; he gives us something that we do not have from any of the others."

Anabben frowned. He stood, causing the others to stare up

at him as he paced. "Would you ever ask one of your fathers for a place to watch one of *my* readings?" he said.

Torephes looked at the other guests for help. It was obvious to Anabben that the young man was humiliated. "This was a special case. Phioth does not perform often."

Anabben said nothing. He went to the dispenser, aware of a buzz of whispered conversation behind his back. Knowing that the young man would not dare ask twice, he had TECT lower the temperature another fifteen degrees.

"Our friend Briol wanted to be a writer," said Anabben, after he returned to his place with a cup of stimulant. "He was one of the lucky ones. I'm not sure what arguments your fathers have used, but they can't know the truths of the matter unless they're writers, too."

"I wish that I'd known what it was going to be like before I tried it," said Briol with a nervous laugh. "There's a good chance that I wouldn't have done it."

"And if you hadn't gone before Stalele . . ." said Rochei.

Anabben put down his cup and grasped Torephes' arm. "You ought to listen. We're going to tell you about what it's like, and what just might happen to you, and if you still want to be a writer, we'll know you're insane."

"Don't listen to him, Torephes," said Charait. "I feel responsible. I brought you here. Perhaps it was a bad idea. Anabben's tired."

"No, no," said Anabben. "Not at all. He shouldn't think our life is all glamour and glory."

Torephes tried unsuccessfully to remove his arm from Anabben's hold. "I never had any illusions that way," he said.

"Wait a minute," said Anabben. "I want Briol to tell you about it."

Briol was sitting quietly, his knees drawn up and his head resting on his folded arms. He was older than anyone else in the meeting area, but the writers had their own special style of respect; he was the least experienced writer, and had to

THE GHOST WRITER | 82

accept their inattention without offense. "Well," said Briol slowly, "the first time was very frightening. I put my thumb in the groove, and I felt a little pinprick. I waited for the relaxant to take effect and then I just had TECT send me. I mean, out. Instead of to a place. Even with the drug I was still afraid."

Briol stared at the softly lighted grass as he spoke. He was an elderly man, one who had lived a useful life as a citizen, and his reasons for becoming a writer at such an advanced age were his secret. "For a brief, bright second there was a glimpse of the death stream itself," he said, his voice growing hoarse. "But before my mind could, well, sicken, I guess, I was rescued by the dead self of a person I know as Daniel Defoe. I was very lucky. That was my audition."

"And your first performance?" asked Torephes.

Briol looked up and smiled. "I was still afraid," he said. "I was afraid that this time Daniel Defoe wouldn't be there. But he was. And he always will be. For me."

"Tell him about Stalele," said Anabben, getting up for another cup of stimulant.

Briol said nothing. "Was he the one who auditioned after you?" asked Tradenne. Briol nodded.

"Did he fail?" asked Torephes.

"It was the most horrible thing I've ever seen," said Vakeis.

"Do you want to try?" asked Anabben, sitting down next to Rochei.

Torephes took Vakeis' hand. "Yes," he said.

Anabben laughed. "Good," he said. "Wonderful. Perhaps you'll land Homer."

"Don't joke with him, Anabben," said Vakeis. "He doesn't understand his chances."

"Oh, he knows the risks," said Anabben. "Come on, let's get it over with. We'll all meet on the stage of the stadium." He rose first, and disappeared into his private tect. The others followed, and TECT transported them to the vast, empty arena.

"Shall we have light?" asked Anabben.

"I suppose," said Torephes.

Anabben requested light from TECT, and the stadium was flooded with a bright noonday glow. "Don't be afraid," said Anabben, leading Torephes to the chair. "Briol is an old man. Death thoughts are his business. Why don't you think of Vakeis? If you come back with a good one, she may be yours."

"I may be his already," said Vakeis sourly. "Why don't you show him what to do?"

Anabben stared at her angrily. "I gave my performance today," he said at last. "My mind is exhausted."

"That's all right," said Torephes. He sat in the chair, bending down to inspect the arm that contained the relaxant pin. "I put my thumb here?" he asked.

"Yes," said Charait. "But you don't have to do this tonight, you know. Your fathers agreed to let me bring you to meet the others. I don't know if they mean for you to try your skill so soon."

"I'll take the responsibility," said Anabben. "He looks like a bright, intense boy."

"I . . . I did it," said Torephes. "How long . . ."

"You should feel it already," said Rochei softly.

"Yes."

"Now have TECT send you," said Briol. "Just as if you were going to the stadium, or to school, but don't specify a place. Just . . . *away.*"

There was a short silence. Then Torephes' eyes grew wide; his mouth opened, but he made no sound other than a quiet gurgling. His lips drew back in a terrified snarl. His fists clenched, and he half stood up in the chair, his neck muscles straining and his back arched tensely.

Vakeis gasped, and hid her eyes on Charait's shoulder. Before anyone could say a word three tectmen had arrived and had *made* Torephes *away* through the small tect at the edge of the stage.

"No one home," said Anabben.

"That poor young boy," said Tradenne.

"He was a fool," said Anabben. "He got what he deserved. He wanted glory, but he didn't want to work. Just to parrot the rotting words of some ancient ghost."

"Don't you pity him?" asked Rochei.

"No, I don't. He knew what might happen."

"But we all started like him," said Charait. "We all take that chance. You can't blame *him;* you did it yourself once."

"No, I didn't," said Anabben quietly.

The others looked puzzled. Anabben frowned; if he explained now he would be doing a service, he thought. There need never be another Stalele, another Torephes.

"Don't you see?" he said. "All of you, fishing in the wild streams of death for a shred here and a tatter there. But everything you find belongs with the dead, with the dead worlds of thousands of years ago. But not me. Don't you see? For the first time in scores of centuries, someone is creating. I don't merely report, I *write*. There never was a Sandor Courane. His words are from *my* mind."

Vakeis began to cry. Charait grabbed Anabben's wrists. "You are saying that you do not have TECT send you?" he asked.

"No," said Anabben defiantly. "I have never tried."

"Then you've lied?" asked Tradenne.

"I cannot comprehend," said Briol. "You are not performing those bits of fiction? You are speaking them yourself? I cannot comprehend."

Anabben looked from one person to the other. In the strange light in the stadium each face seemed incredulous and afraid. "Don't you understand?" shouted Anabben. "I do it myself!"

They moved away from Anabben, leaving him by the empty chair. He looked wildly for some sign of approval, of awed surprise, but found only loathing. He started to scream, but stopped when Tradenne raised a hand.

"You are very *different*," said the old man. Before he finished speaking three tectmen had appeared to *make* Anabben *away*.

MANY MANSIONS

by Robert Silverberg

Robert Silverberg has appeared in each number of Universe, *with a series of stories that combine the sense of wonder with a sense of humor. He won a Nebula Award for his first story in this series, "Good News from the Vatican." In this new novelette he explores the infinite possibilities for human absurdity that are offered by time travel and alternate time tracks. You think you've seen all the variations on the go-back-in-time-and-kill-your-grandfather plot? But they're literally endless . . .*

IT'S BEEN a rough day. Everything gone wrong. A tremendous tie-up on the freeway going to work, two accounts canceled before lunch, now some inconceivable botch by the weather programmers. It's snowing outside. Actually snowing. He'll have to go out and clear the driveway in the morning. He can't remember when it last snowed. And of course a fight with Alice again. She never lets him alone. She's at her most deadly when she sees him come home exhausted from the office. Ted, why don't you this; Ted, get me that. Now, waiting for dinner, working on his third drink in forty minutes, he feels one of his headaches coming on. Those miserable killer headaches that can destroy a whole evening. What a life! He toys with murderous fantasies. Take her out by the reservoir for a friendly little stroll, give her a quick hard shove with his shoulder. She can't swim. Down, down, down. Glub. Goodbye, Alice. Free at last.

In the kitchen she furiously taps the keys of the console, programming dinner just the way he likes it. Cold vichyssoise, baked potato with sour cream and chives, sirloin steak blood-rare inside and charcoal-charred outside. Don't think it isn't work to get the meal just right, even with the autochef. All for him. The bastard. Tell me, why do I sweat so hard to please him? Has he made me happy? What's he ever done for me except waste the best years of my life? And he thinks I don't know about his other women. Those lunchtime quickies. Oh, I wouldn't mind at all if he dropped dead tomorrow. I'd be a great widow—so dignified at the funeral, so strong, hardly crying at all. And everybody thinks we're such a close couple. "Married eleven years and they're still in love." I heard someone say that only last week. If they only knew the truth about us. If they only knew.

Martin peers out the window of his third-floor apartment in Sunset Village. Snow. I'll be damned. He can't remember the last time he saw snow. Thirty, forty years back, maybe, when Ted was a baby. He absolutely can't remember. White stuff on the ground—when? The mind gets wobbly when you're past eighty. He still can't believe he's an old man. It rocks him to realize that his grandson Ted, Martha's boy, is almost forty. I bounced that kid on my knee and he threw up all over my suit. Four years old then. Nixon was President. Nobody talks much about Tricky Dick these days. Ancient history. McKinley, Coolidge, Nixon. Time flies. Martin thinks of Ted's wife Alice. What a nice tight little ass she has. What a cute pair of jugs. I'd like to get my hands on them. I really would. You know something, Martin? You're not such an old ruin yet. Not if you can get it up for your grandson's wife.

His dreams of drowning her fade as quickly as they came. He is not a violent man by nature. He knows he could never do it. He can't even bring himself to step on a spider; how then could he kill his wife? If she'd die some other way, of course, without the need of his taking direct action, that would solve everything. She's driving to the hairdresser on one of those manual-access roads she likes to use and her car swerves on an icy spot, and she goes into a tree at eighty kilometers an hour. Good. She's shopping on Union Boulevard and the bank is blown up by an activist; she's nailed by flying debris. Good. The dentist gives her a new anesthetic and it turns out she's fatally allergic to it. Puffs up like a blowfish and dies in five minutes. Good. The police come— long faces, snuffly noses. Terribly sorry, Mr. Porter. There's been an awful accident. Don't tell me it's my wife, he cries. They nod lugubriously. He bears up bravely under the loss, though.

"You can come in for dinner now," she says. He's sitting slouched on the sofa with another drink in his hand. He drinks more than any man she knows—not that she knows all that many. Maybe he'll get cirrhosis and die. Do people still die of cirrhosis, she wonders, or do they give them liver transplants now? The funny thing is that he still turns her on, after eleven years. His eyes, his face, his hands. She despises him, but he still turns her on.

The snow reminds him of his young manhood, of his days long ago in the East. He was quite the ladies' man then. And it wasn't so easy to get some action back in those days, either. The girls were always worried about what people would say if anyone found out. *What people would say!* As if doing it with a boy you liked was something shameful. Or they'd worry about getting knocked up. They made you wear a rubber. How awful that was: like wearing a sock. The pill was just starting to come in, the original pill, the old one-a-day kind. Imagine a world without the pill! ("Did they have dinosaurs when you were a boy, Grandpa?") Still, Martin had made out all right. Big muscular frame, strong earnest features, warm inquisitive eyes. You'd never know it to look at me now. I wonder if Alice realizes what kind of stud I used to be. If I had the money I'd rent one of those time machines they've got now and send her back to visit myself around 1950 or so. A little gift to my younger self. He'd really rip into her. It gives Martin a quick riffle of excitement to think of his younger self ripping into Alice. But of course he can't afford any such thing.

As he forks down his steak he imagines being single again. Would I get married again? Not on your life. Not until I'm good and ready, anyway; maybe when I'm fifty-five or sixty. Me for bachelorhood for the time being, just screwing around like a kid. To hell with responsibilities. I'll wait two, three weeks after the funeral, a decent interval, and then I'll go off for some fun. Hawaii, Tahiti, Fiji, someplace out there. With Nolie. Or Maria. Or Ellie. Yes, with Ellie. He thinks of Ellie's pink thighs, her soft heavy breasts, her long, radiant, auburn hair. Two weeks in Fiji with Ellie. Two weeks in Ellie with Fiji. Yes. Yes. Yes. "Is the steak rare enough for you, Ted?" Alice asks. "It's fine," he says.

She goes upstairs to check the children's bedroom. They're both asleep, finally. Or else faking it so well that it makes no difference. She stands by their beds a moment, thinking, I love you, Bobby, I love you, Tink. Tink and Bobby, Bobby and Tink. I love you even though you drive me crazy sometimes. She tiptoes out. Now for a quiet evening of television. And then to bed. The same old routine. Christ. I don't know why I go on like this. There are times when I'm ready to explode. I stay with him for the children's sake, I guess. Is that enough of a reason?

He envisions himself running hand in hand along the beach with Ellie. Both of them naked, their skins bronzed and gleaming in the tropical sunlight. Palm trees everywhere. Grains of pink sand under foot. Soft, transparent wavelets lapping the shore. A quiet cove. "No one can see us here," Ellie murmurs. He sinks down on her firm, sleek body and enters her.

A blazing band of pain tightens like a strip of hot metal across Martin's chest. He staggers away from the window, dropping into a low crouch as he stumbles toward a chair. The heart. Oh, the heart! That's what you get for drooling over Alice. Dirty old man. "Help," he calls feebly. "Come on, you filthy machine, help me!" The medic, activated by the key phrase, rolls silently toward him. Its sensors are already at work scanning him, searching for the cause of the discomfort. A telescoping steel-jacketed arm slides out of the medic's chest and, hovering above Martin, extrudes an ultrasonic injection snout. "Yes," Martin murmurs, "that's right, damn you, hurry up and give me the drug!" Calm. I must try to remain calm. The snout makes a gentle whirring noise as it forces the relaxant into Martin's vein. He slumps in relief. The pain slowly ebbs. Oh, that's much better. Saved again. Oh. Oh. Oh. Dirty old man. Ought to be ashamed of yourself.

Ted knows he won't get to Fiji with Ellie or anybody else. Any realistic assessment of the situation brings him inevitably to the same conclusion. Alice isn't going to die in an accident, any more than he's likely to murder her. She'll live forever. Unwanted wives always do. He could ask for a divorce, of course. He'd probably lose everything he owned, but he'd win his freedom. Or he could simply do away with himself. That was always a temptation for him. The easy way out; no lawyers, no hassles. So it's that time of the evening again. It's the same every night. Pretending to watch television, he secretly indulges in suicidal fantasies.

Bare-bodied dancers in gaudy luminous paint gyrate lasciviously on the screen, nearly large as life. Alice scowls. The things they show on TV nowadays! It used to be that you got this stuff only on the X-rated channels, but now it's everywhere. And look at him, just lapping it up! Actually she knows she wouldn't be so stuffy about the sex shows except that Ted's fascination with them is a measure of his lack of interest in her. Let them show screwing and all the rest on TV, if that's what people want. I just wish Ted had as much enthusiasm for me as he does for the television stuff. So far as sexual permissiveness in general goes, she's no prude. She used to wear nothing but trunks at the beach until Tink was born and she started to feel a little less proud of her figure. But she still dresses as revealingly as anyone in their crowd. And gets stared at by everyone but her own husband. *He* watches the TV cuties. His other women must use him up. Maybe I ought to step out a bit myself, Alice thinks. She's had her little affairs along the way. Not many, nothing very serious, but she's had some. Three lovers in eleven years: that's not a great many, but it's a sign that she's no puritan. She wonders if she ought to get involved with somebody now. It might move her life off dead center while she still has the chance, before boredom destroys her entirely. "I'm going up to wash my hair," she announces. "Will you be staying down here till bedtime?"

There are so many ways he could do it. Slit his wrists. Drive his car off the bridge. Swallow Alice's whole box of sleeping tabs. Of course, those are all old-fashioned ways of killing yourself. Something more modern would be appropriate. Go into one of the black taverns and start making loud racial insults? No, nothing modern about that. It's very 1975. But something genuinely contemporary does occur to him. Those time machines they've got now: suppose he rented one and went back, say, sixty years, to a time when one of his parents hadn't yet been born. And killed his grandfather. Find old Martin as a young man and slip a knife into him. If I do that, Ted figures, I should instantly and painlessly cease to exist. I would never have existed, because my mother wouldn't ever have existed. Poof. Out like a light. Then he realizes he's fantasizing a murder again. Stupid—if he could ever murder anyone, he'd murder Alice and be done with it. So the whole fantasy is foolish. Back to the starting point is where he is.

She is sitting under the hair drier when he comes upstairs. He has a peculiarly smug expression on his face, and as soon as she turns the drier off she asks him what he's thinking about. "I may have just invented a perfect murder method," he tells her. "Oh?" she says. He says, "You rent a time machine. Then you go back a couple of generations and murder one of the ancestors of your intended victim. That way you're murdering the victim too, because he won't ever have been born if you kill off one of his immediate progenitors. Then you return to your own time. Nobody can trace you because you don't have any fingerprints on file in an era before your own birth. What do you think of it?" Alice shrugs. "It's an old one," she says. "It's been done on television a dozen times. Anyway, I don't like it. Why should an innocent person have to die just because he's the grandparent of somebody you want to kill?"

They're probably in bed together right now, Martin thinks gloomily. Stark naked side by side. The lights are out. The house is quiet. Maybe they're smoking a little grass. Do they still call it grass, he wonders, or is there some new nickname now? Anyway, the two of them turn on. Yes. And then he reaches for her. His hands slide over her cool smooth skin. He cups her breasts. Plays with the hard little nipples. Sucks on them. The other hand wandering down to her parted thighs. And then she. And then he. And then they. And then they. Oh, Alice, he murmurs. Oh, Ted, *Ted*, she cries. And then they. Go to it. Up and down, in and out. Oh. Oh. Oh. She claws his back. She pumps her hips. Ted! Ted! Ted! The big moment is arriving now. For her, for him. Jackpot! Afterward they lie close for a few minutes, basking in the afterglow. And then they roll apart. Good night, Ted. Good night, Alice. Oh, Jesus. They do it every night, I bet. They're so young and full of juice. And I'm all dried up. Christ, I hate being old. When I think of the man I once was. When I think of the women I once had. Jesus. Jesus. God, let me have the strength to do it just once more before I die. And leave me alone for two hours with Alice.

She has trouble falling asleep. A strange scene keeps playing itself out obsessively in her mind. She sees herself stepping out of an upright coffin-sized box of dark gray metal, festooned with dials and levers. The time machine. It delivers her into a dark, dirty alleyway, and when she walks forward to the street she sees scores of little antique automobiles buzzing around. Only they aren't antiques: they're the current models. This is the year 1947. New York City. Will she be conspicuous in her futuristic clothes? She has her breasts covered, at any rate. That's essential back here. She hurries to the proper address, resisting the temptation to browse in shop windows along the way. How quaint and ancient everything looks. And how dirty the streets are. She comes to a tall building of red brick. This is the place. No scanners study her as she enters. They don't have annunciators yet or any other automatic home-protection equipment. She goes upstairs in an elevator so creaky and unstable that she fears for her life. Fifth floor. Apartment 5-J. She rings the doorbell. *He* answers. He's terribly young, only twenty-four, but she can pick out signs of the Martin of the future in his face, the strong cheekbones, the searching blue eyes. "Are you Martin Jamieson?" she asks. "That's right," he says. She smiles. "May I come in?" "Of course," he says. He bows her into the apartment. As he momentarily turns his back on her to open the coat closet she takes the heavy steel pipe from her purse and lifts it high and brings it down on the back of his head. *Thwock.* She takes the heavy steel pipe from her purse and lifts it high and brings it down on the back of his head. *Thwock.* She takes the heavy steel pipe from her purse and lifts it high and brings it down on the back of his head. *Thwock.*

Ted and Alice visit him at Sunset Village two or three times a month. He can't complain about that; it's as much as he can expect. He's an old, old man and no doubt a boring one, but they come dutifully, sometimes with the kids, sometimes without. He's never gotten used to the idea that he's a great-grandfather. Alice always gives him a kiss when she arrives and another when she leaves. He plays a private little game with her, copping a feel at each kiss. His hand quickly stroking her butt. Or sometimes when he's really rambunctious his hand travels lightly over her breasts. Does she notice? Probably. She never lets on, though. Pretends it's an accidental touch. Most likely she thinks it's charming that a man of his age would still have at least a vestige of sexual desire left. Unless she thinks it's disgusting, that is.

The time-machine gimmick, Ted tells himself, can be used in ways that don't quite amount to murder. For instance. "What's that box?" Alice asks. He smiles cunningly. "It's called a panchronicon," he says. "It gives you a kind of televised reconstruction of ancient times. The salesman loaned me a demonstration sample." She says, "How does it work?" "Just step inside," he tells her. "It's all ready for you." She starts to enter the machine, but then, suddenly suspicious, she hesitates on the threshold. He pushes her in and slams the door shut behind her. *Wham!* The controls are set. Off goes Alice on a one-way journey to the Pleistocene. The machine is primed to return as soon as it drops her off. That isn't murder, is it? She's still alive, wherever she may be, unless the saber-toothed tigers have caught up with her. So long, Alice.

In the morning she drives Bobby and Tink to school. Then she stops at the bank and the post office. From ten to eleven she has her regular session at the identity-reinforcement parlor. Ordinarily she would go right home after that, but this morning she strolls across the shopping-center plaza to the office that the time-machine people have just opened. TEMPONAUTICS, LTD., the sign over the door says. The place is empty except for two machines, no doubt demonstration models, and a bland-faced, smiling salesman. "Hello," Alice says nervously. "I just wanted to pick up some information about the rental costs of one of your machines."

Martin likes to imagine Alice coming to visit him by herself some rainy Saturday afternoon. "Ted isn't able to make it today," she explains. "Something came up at the office. But I knew you were expecting us, and I didn't want you to be disappointed. Poor Martin, you must lead such a lonely life." She comes close to him. She is trembling. So is he. Her face is flushed and her eyes are bright with the unmistakable glossiness of desire. He feels a sense of sexual excitement too, for the first time in ten or twenty years, that tension in the loins, that throbbing of the pulse. Electricity. Chemistry. His eyes lock on hers. Her nostrils flare, her mouth goes taut. "Martin," she whispers huskily. "Do you feel what I feel?" "You know I do," he tells her. She says, "If only I could have known you when you were in your prime!" He chuckles. "I'm not altogether senile yet," he cries exultantly. Then she is in his arms and his lips are seeking her fragrant breasts.

"Yes, it came as a terrible shock to me," Ted tells Ellie. "Having her disappear like that. She simply vanished from the face of the earth, as far as anyone can determine. They've tried every possible way of tracing her and there hasn't been a clue." Ellie's flawless forehead furrows in a fitful frown. "Was she unhappy?" she asks. "Do you think she may have done away with herself?" Ted shakes his head. "I don't know. You live with a person for eleven years and you think you know her pretty well, and then one day something absolutely incomprehensible occurs and you realize how impossible it is ever to know another human being at all. Don't you agree?" Ellie nods gravely. "Yes, oh, yes, certainly!" she says. He smiles down at her and takes her hands in his. Softly he says, "Let's not talk about Alice any more, shall we? She's gone and that's all I'll ever know." He hears a pulsing symphonic crescendo of shimmering angelic choirs as he embraces her and murmurs, "I love you, Ellie. I love you."

She takes the heavy steel pipe from her purse and lifts it high and brings it down on the back of his head. *Thwock*. Young Martin drops instantly, twitches once, lies still. Dark blood begins to seep through the dense blond curls of his hair. How strange to see Martin with golden hair, she thinks as she kneels beside his body. She puts her hand to the bloody place, probes timidly, feels the deep indentation. Is he dead? She isn't sure how to tell. He isn't moving. He doesn't seem to be breathing. She wonders if she ought to hit him again, just to make certain. Then she remembers something she's seen on television, and takes her mirror from her purse. Holds it in front of his face. No cloud forms. That's pretty conclusive: you're dead, Martin. R.I.P. Martin Jamieson, 1923–1947. Which means that Martha Jamieson Porter (1948–   ) will never now be conceived, and that automatically obliterates the existence of her son Theodore Porter (1968–   ). Not bad going, Alice, getting rid of unloved husband and miserable shrewish mother-in-law all in one shot. Sorry, Martin. Bye-bye, Ted. (R.I.P. Theodore Porter, 1968–1947. Eh?) She rises, goes into the bathroom with the steel pipe, and carefully rinses it off. Then she puts it back into her purse. Now to go back to the machine and return to 2006, she thinks. To start my new life. But as she leaves the apartment, a tall, lean man steps out of the hallway shadows and clamps his hand powerfully around her wrist. "Time Patrol," he says crisply, flashing an identification badge. "You're under arrest for temponautic murder, Mrs. Porter."

Today has been a better day than yesterday, low on crises and depressions, but he still feels a headache coming on as he lets himself into the house. He is braced for whatever bitchiness Alice may have in store for him this evening. But she seems oddly relaxed and amiable. "Can I get you a drink, Ted?" she asks. "How did your day go?" He smiles and says, "Well, I think we may have salvaged the Hammond account after all. Otherwise nothing special happened. And you? What did you do today, love?" She shrugs. "Oh, the usual stuff," she says. "The bank, the post office, my identity-reinforcement session."

If you had the money, Martin asks himself, how far back would you send her? 1947, that would be the year, I guess. My last year as a single man. No sense complicating things. Off you go, Alice baby, to 1947. Let's make it March. By June I was engaged and by September Martha was on the way, though I didn't find that out until later. Yes: March, 1947. So. Young Martin answers the doorbell and sees an attractive girl in the hall—a woman, really, older than he is, maybe thirty or thirty-two. Slender, dark-haired, nicely constructed. Odd clothing: a clinging gray tunic, very short, made of some strange fabric that flows over her body like a stream. How it achieves that liquid effect around the pleats is beyond him. "Are you Martin Jamieson?" she asks. And quickly answers herself. "Yes, of course, you must be. I recognize you. How handsome you were!" He is baffled. He knows nothing, naturally, about this gift from his aged future self. "Who are you?" he asks. "May I come in first?" she says. He is embarrassed by his lack of courtesy and waves her inside. Her eyes glitter with mischief. "You aren't going to believe this," she tells him, "but I'm your grandson's wife."

"Would you like to try out one of our demonstration models?" the salesman asks pleasantly. "There's absolutely no cost or obligation." Ted looks at Alice. Alice looks at Ted. Her frown mirrors his inner uncertainty. She too must be wishing that they had never come to the Temponautics showroom. The salesman, pattering smoothly onward, says, "In these demonstrations we usually send our potential customers fifteen or twenty minutes into the past. I'm sure you'll find it fascinating. While remaining in the machine, you'll be able to look through a viewer and observe your own selves actually entering this very showroom a short while ago. Well? Will you give it a try? You go first, Mrs. Porter. I assure you it's going to be the most unique experience you've ever had." Alice, uneasy, tries to back off, but the salesman prods her in a way that is at once gentle and unyielding, and she steps reluctantly into the time machine. He closes the door. A great business of adjusting fine controls ensues. Then the salesman throws a master switch. A green glow envelops the machine and it disappears, although something transparent and vague—a retinal afterimage? the ghost of the machine? —remains dimly visible. The salesman says, "She's now gone a short distance into her own past. I've programmed the machine to take her back eighteen minutes and keep her there for a total elapsed interval of six minutes, so she can see the entire opening moments of your visit here. But when I return her to Now Level, there's no need to match the amount of elapsed time in the past, so that from our point of view she'll have been absent only some thirty seconds. Isn't that remarkable, Mr. Porter? It's one of the many extraordinary paradoxes we encounter in the strange new realm of time travel." He throws another switch. The time machine once more assumes solid form. *"Voilá!"* cries the salesman. "Here is Mrs. Porter, returned safe and sound from her voyage into the past." He flings open the door of the time machine. The passenger compartment is empty. The salesman's face crumbles. "Mrs. Porter?" he shrieks in consternation. "Mrs. Porter? I don't understand! How could there have been a malfunction? This is impossible! Mrs. Porter? *Mrs. Porter?"*

She hurries down the dirty street toward the tall brick building. This is the place. Upstairs. Fifth floor, Apartment 5-J. As she starts to ring the doorbell, a tall, lean man steps out of the shadows and clamps his hand powerfully around her wrist. "Time Patrol," he says crisply, flashing an identification badge. "You're under arrest for contemplated temponautic murder, Mrs. Porter."

"But I haven't any grandson," he sputters. "I'm not even mar—" She laughs. "Don't worry about it!" she tells him. "You're going to have a daughter named Martha and she'll have a son named Ted and I'm going to marry Ted and we'll have two children named Bobby and Tink. And you're going to live to be an old, old man. And that's all you need to know. Now let's have a little fun." She touches a catch at the side of her tunic and the garment falls away in a single fluid cascade. Beneath it she is naked. Her nipples stare up at him like blind pink eyes. She beckons to him. "Come on!" she says hoarsely. "Get undressed, Martin! You're wasting time!"

Alice giggles nervously. "Well, as a matter of fact," she says to the salesman, "I think I'm willing to let my husband be the guinea pig. How about it, Ted?" She turns toward him. So does the salesman. "Certainly, Mr. Porter. I know you're eager to give our machine a test run, yes?" No, Ted thinks, but he feels the pressure of events propelling him willy-nilly. He gets into the machine. As the door closes on him he fears that claustrophobic panic will overwhelm him; he is reassured by the sight of a handle on the door's inner face. He pushes on it and the door opens, and he steps out of the machine just in time to see his earlier self coming into the Temponautics showroom with Alice. The salesman is going forward to greet them. Ted is now eighteen minutes into his own past. Alice and the other Ted stare at him, aghast. The salesman whirls and exclaims, "Wait a second, you aren't supposed to get out of—" How stupid they all look! How bewildered! Ted laughs in their faces. Then he rushes past them, nearly knocking his other self down, and erupts into the shopping-center plaza. He sprints in a wild frenzy of exhilaration toward the parking area. Free, he thinks. I'm free at last. And I didn't have to kill anybody.

Suppose I rent a machine, Alice thinks, and go back to 1947 and kill Martin. Suppose I really do it. What if there's some way of tracing the crime to me? After all, a crime committed by a person from 2006 who goes back to 1947 will have consequences in our present day. It might change all sorts of things. So they'd want to catch the criminal and punish him, or better yet prevent the crime from being committed in the first place. And the time-machine company is bound to know what year I asked them to send me to. So maybe it isn't such an easy way of committing a perfect crime. I don't know. God, I can't understand any of this. But perhaps I can get away with it. Anyway, I'm going to give it a try. I'll show Ted he can't go on treating me like dirt.

They lie peacefully side by side, sweaty, drowsy, exhausted in the good exhaustion that comes after a first-rate screw. Martin tenderly strokes her belly and thighs. How smooth her skin is, how pale, how transparent! The little blue veins so clearly visible. "Hey," he says suddenly. "I just thought of something. I wasn't wearing a rubber or anything. What if I made you pregnant? And if you're really who you say you are, then you'll go back to the year 2006 and you'll have a kid and he'll be his own grandfather, won't he?" She laughs. "Don't worry much about it," she says.

A wave of timidity comes over her as she enters the Temponautics office. This is crazy, she tells herself. I'm get-

ting out of here. But before she can turn around, the salesman she spoke to the day before materializes from a side
room and gives her a big hello. Mr. Friesling. He's practically
rubbing his hands together in anticipation of landing a contract. "So nice to see you again, Mrs. Porter." She nods and
glances worriedly at the demonstration models. "How much
would it cost," she asks, "to spend a few hours in the spring
of 1947?"

Sunday is the big family day. Four generations sitting
down to dinner together: Martin, Martha, Ted and Alice,
Bobby and Tink. Ted rather enjoys these reunions, but he
knows Alice loathes them, mainly because of Martha. Alice
hates her mother-in-law. Martha has never cared much for
Alice, either. He watches them glaring at each other across
the table. Meanwhile, old Martin stares lecherously at the
gulf between Alice's breasts. You have to hand it to the old
man, Ted thinks. He's never lost the old urge. Even though
there's not a hell of a lot he can do about gratifying it, not at
his age. Martha says sweetly, "You'd look ever so much better, Alice dear, if you'd let your hair grow out to its natural
color." A sugary smile from Martha. A sour scowl from Alice.
She glowers at the older woman. "This *is* its natural color,"
she snaps.

Mr. Friesling hands her the standard contract form.
Eight pages of densely packed type. "Don't be frightened by
it, Mrs. Porter. It looks formidable, but actually it's just a lot
of empty legal rhetoric. You can show it to your lawyer, if you
like. I can tell you, though, that most of our customers find
no need for that." She leafs through it. So far as she can tell,
the contract is mainly a disclaimer of responsibility. Temponautics, Ltd., agrees to bear the brunt of any malfunction
caused by its own demonstrable negligence, but wants no
truck with acts of God or with accidents brought about by

clients who won't obey the safety regulations. On the fourth page Alice finds a clause warning the prospective renter that the company cannot be held liable for any consequences of actions by the renter which wantonly or willfully interfere with the already determined course of history. She translates that for herself: *If you kill your husband's grandfather, don't blame us if you get in trouble.* She skims the remaining pages. "It looks harmless enough," she says. "Where do I sign?"

As Martin comes out of the bathroom he finds Martha blocking his way. "Excuse me," he says mildly, but she remains in his path. She is a big fleshy woman. At fifty-eight she affects the fashions of the very young, with grotesque results; he hates that aspect of her. He can see why Alice dislikes her so much. "Just a moment," Martha says. "I want to talk to you, Father." "About what?" he asks. "About those looks you give Alice. Don't you think that's a little too much? How tasteless can you get?" "Tasteless? Are you anybody to talk about taste, with your face painted green like a fifteen-year-old?" She looks angry: he's scored a direct hit. She replies, "I just think that at the age of eighty-two you ought to have a greater regard for decency than to go staring down your own grandson's wife's front." Martin sighs. "Let me have the staring, Martha. It's all I've got left."

He is at the office, deep in complicated negotiations, when his autosecretary bleeps him and announces that a call has come in from a Mr. Friesling, of the Union Boulevard Plaza office of Temponautics, Ltd. Ted is puzzled by that: What do the time-machine people want with him? Trying to line him up as a customer? "Tell him I'm not interested in time trips," Ted says. But the autosecretary bleeps again a few moments later. Mr. Friesling, it declares, is calling in reference to Mr. Porter's credit standing. More baffled than before, Ted orders the call switched over to him. Mr. Friesling appears on the desk screen. He is small-featured and bright-eyed, rather like a chipmunk. "I apologize for troubling you, Mr. Porter," he begins. "This is strictly a routine credit check, but it's altogether necessary. As you surely know, your wife has requested rental of our equipment for a fifty-nine-year time jaunt, and inasmuch as the service fee for such a trip exceeds the level at which we extend automatic credit, our policy requires me to ask you if you'll confirm the payment schedule that she has requested us to—" Ted coughs violently. "Hold on," he says. "My wife's going on a time jaunt? What the hell, this is the first time I've heard of that!"

She is surprised by the extensiveness of the preparations. No wonder they charge so much. Getting her ready for the jaunt takes hours. They inoculate her to protect her against certain extinct diseases. They provide her with clothing in the style of the mid-twentieth century, ill-fitting and uncomfortable. They give her contemporary currency, but warn her that she would do well not to spend any except in an emergency, since she will be billed for it at its present-day numismatic value, which is high. They make her study a pamphlet describing the customs and historical background of the era and quiz her in detail. She learns that she is not under any circumstances to expose her breasts or genitals in public while she is in 1947. She must not attempt to obtain any mind-stimulating drugs other than alcohol. She should not say anything that might be construed as praise of the Soviet Union or of Marxist philosophy. She must bear in mind that she is entering the past solely as an observer, and should engage in minimal social interaction with the citizens of the era she is visiting. And so forth. At last they decide it's safe to let her go. "Please come this way, Mrs. Porter," Friesling says.

After staring at the telephone a long while, Martin punches out Alice's number. Before the second ring he loses his nerve and disconnects. Immediately he calls her again. His heart pounds so furiously that the medic, registering alarm on its delicate sensing apparatus, starts toward him. He waves the robot away and clings to the phone. Two rings. Three. Ah. "Hello?" Alice says. Her voice is warm and rich and feminine. He has his screen switched off. "Hello? Who's there?" Martin breathes heavily into the mouthpiece. Ah. Ah. Ah. Ah. "Hello? Hello? Hello? Listen, you pervert, if you phone me once more—" *Ah. Ah. Ah.* A smile of bliss appears on Martin's withered features. Alice hangs up. Trembling, Martin sags in his chair. Oh, that was good! He signals fiercely to the medic. "Let's have the injection now, you metal monster!" He laughs. Dirty old man.

Ted realizes that it isn't necessary to kill a person's grandfather in order to get rid of that person. Just interfere with some crucial event in that person's past, is all. Go back and break up the marriage of Alice's grandparents, for example. (How? Seduce the grandmother when she's eighteen? "I'm terribly sorry to inform you that your intended bride is no virgin, and here's the documentary evidence." They were very grim about virginity back then, weren't they?) Nobody would have to die. But Alice wouldn't ever be born.

Martin still can't believe any of this, even after she's slept with him. It's some crazy practical joke, most likely. Although he wishes all practical jokes were as sexy as this one. "Are you really from the year 2006?" he asks her. She laughs prettily. "How can I prove it to you?" Then she leaps from the bed. He tracks her with his eyes as she crosses the room, breasts jiggling gaily. What a sweet little body. How thoughtful of my older self to ship her back here to me. If that's what really happened. She fumbles in her purse and extracts a handful of coins. "Look here," she says. "Money from the future. Here's a dime from 1993. And this is a two-dollar piece from 2001. And here's an old one, a 1979 Kennedy half dollar." He studies the unfamiliar coins. They have a greasy look, not silvery at all. Counterfeits? They won't necessarily be striking coins out of silver forever. And the engraving job is very professional. A two-dollar piece, eh? Well, you never can tell. And this. The half dollar. A handsome young man in profile. "Kennedy?" he says. "Who's Kennedy?"

So this is it at last. Two technicians in gray smocks watch her, sober-faced, as she clambers into the machine. It's very much like a coffin, just as she imagined it would be. She can't sit down in it; it's too narrow. Gives her the creeps, shut up in here. Of course, they've told her the trip won't take any apparent subjective time, only a couple of seconds. *Woosh!* and she'll be there. All right. They close the door. She hears the lock clicking shut. Mr. Friesling's voice comes to her over a loudspeaker. "We wish you a happy voyage, Mrs. Porter. Keep calm and you won't get into any difficulties." Suddenly the red light over the door is glowing. That means the jaunt has begun: she's traveling backward in time. No sense of acceleration, no sense of motion. One, two, three. The light goes off. That's it. I'm in 1947, she tells herself. Before she opens the door, she closes her eyes and runs through her history lessons. World War II has just ended. Europe is in ruins. There are forty-eight states. Nobody has been to the moon yet or even thinks much about going there. Harry Truman is President. Stalin runs Russia and Churchill—is Churchill still Prime Minister of England? She isn't sure. Well, no matter. I didn't come here to talk about prime ministers. She touches the latch, and the door of the time machine swings outward.

He steps from the machine into the year 2006. Nothing has changed in the showroom. Friesling, the two poker-faced technicians, the sleek desks, the thick carpeting —all the same as before. He moves bouncily. His mind is still back there with Alice's grandmother. The taste of her lips, the soft urgent cries of her fulfillment. Who ever said all women were frigid in the old days? They ought to go back and find out. Friesling smiles at him. "I hope you had a very enjoyable journey, Mr. . . . ah—" Ted nods. "Enjoyable and useful," he says. He goes out. Never to see Alice again—how beautiful! The car isn't where he remembers leaving it in the parking area. You have to expect certain small peripheral changes, I guess. He hails a cab, gives the driver his address. His key does not fit the front door. Troubled, he thumbs the annunciator. A woman's voice, not Alice's, asks him what he wants. "Is this the Ted Porter residence?" he asks. "No, it isn't," the woman says, suspicious and irritated. The name on the doorplate, he notices now, is McKenzie. So the changes are not all so small. Where do I go now? If I don't live here, then where? "Wait!" he yells to the taxi, just pulling away. It takes him to a downtown cafe, where he phones Ellie. Her face, peering out of the tiny screen, wears an odd frowning expression. "Listen, something very strange has happened," he begins, "and I need to see you as soon as—" "I don't think I know you," she says. "I'm Ted," he tells her. "Ted who?" she asks.

How peculiar this is, Alice thinks. Like walking into a museum diorama and having it come to life. The noisy little automobiles. The ugly clothing. The squat, dilapidated twentieth-century buildings. The chaos. The oily, smoky smell of the polluted air. Wisps of dirty snow in the streets. Cans of garbage just sitting around as if nobody's ever heard of the plague. Well, I won't stay here long. In her purse she carries her kitchen carver, a tiny nickel-jacketed laser-powered implement. Steel pipes are all right for dream fantasies, but this is the real thing, and she wants the killing to be quick and efficient. Criss, cross, with the laser beam, and Martin goes. At the street corner she pauses to check the address. There's no central info number to ring for all sorts of useful data, not in these primitive times; she must use a printed telephone directory, a thick tattered book with small smeary type. Here he is: Martin Jamieson, 504 West 45th. That's not far. In ten minutes she's there. A dark brick structure, five or six stories high, with spidery metal fire escapes running down its face. Even for its day it appears unusually run down. She goes inside. A list of tenants is posted just within the front door. JAMIESON, 3-A. There's no elevator and of course no liftshaft. Up the stairs. A musty hallway lit by a single dim incandescent bulb. This is Apartment 3-A. Jamieson. She rings the bell.

Ten minutes later Friesling calls back, sounding abashed and looking dismayed: "I'm sorry to have to tell you that there's been some sort of error, Mr. Porter. The technicians were apparently unaware that a credit check was in process and they sent Mrs. Porter off on her trip while we were still talking." Ted is shaken. He clutches the edge of the desk. Controlling himself with an effort, he says, "How far back was it that she wanted to go?" Friesling says, "It was fifty-nine years. To 1947." Ted nods grimly. A horrible idea has occurred to him. 1947 was the year that his mother's parents met and got married. What is Alice up to?

The doorbell rings. Martin, freshly showered, is sprawled out naked on his bed, leafing through the new issue of *Esquire* and thinking vaguely of going out for dinner. He isn't expecting any company. Slipping into his bathrobe, he goes toward the door. "Who's there?" he calls. A youthful, pleasant female voice replies, "I'm looking for Martin Jamieson." Well, okay. He opens the door. She's perhaps twenty-seven, twenty-eight years old, *very* sexy, on the slender side but well-built. Dark hair, worn in a strangely boyish short cut. He's never seen her before. "Hi," he says tentatively. She grins warmly at him. "You don't know me," she tells him, "but I'm a friend of an old friend of yours. Mary Chambers? Mary and I grew up together in, ah, Ohio. I'm visiting New York for the first time, and Mary once told me that if I ever come to New York I should be sure to look up Martin Jamieson, and so—may I come in?" "You bet," he says. He doesn't remember any Mary Chambers from Ohio. But what the hell, sometimes you forget a few. What the hell.

He's much more attractive than she expected him to be. She has always known Martin only as an old man, made unattractive as much by his coarse lechery as by what age has done to him. Hollow-chested, stoop-shouldered, pleated, jowly face, sparse strands of white hair, beady eyes of faded blue—a wreck of a man. But this Martin in the doorway is sturdy, handsome, untouched by time, brimming with life and vigor and virility. She thinks of the carver in her purse and feels a genuine pang of regret at having to cut this robust boy off in his prime. But there isn't such a great hurry, is there? First we can enjoy each other, Martin. And then the laser.

"When is she due back?" Ted demands. Friesling explains that all concepts of time are relative and flexible; so far as elapsed time at Now Level goes, she's already returned. "What?" Ted yells. "Where is she?" Friesling does not know. She stepped out of the machine, bade the Temponautics staff a pleasant goodbye, and left the showroom. Ted puts his hand to his throat. What if she's already killed Martin? Will I just wink out of existence? Or is there some sort of lag, so that I'll fade gradually into unreality over the next few days?

"Listen," he says raggedly, "I'm leaving my office right now and I'll be down at your place in less than an hour. I want you to have your machinery set up so that you can transport me to the exact point in space and time where you just sent my wife." "But that won't be possible," Friesling protests. "It takes hours to prepare a client properly for—" Ted cuts him off. "Get everything set up, and to hell with preparing me properly," he snaps. "Unless you feel like getting slammed with the biggest negligence suit since this time-machine thing got started, you better have everything ready when I get there."

He opens the door. The girl in the hallway is young and good-looking, with close-cropped dark hair and full lips. Thank you, Mary Chambers, whoever you may be. "Pardon the bathrobe," he says, "but I wasn't expecting company." She steps into his apartment. Suddenly he notices how strained and tense her face is. Country girl from Ohio, suddenly having second thoughts about visiting a strange man in a strange city? He tries to put her at her ease. "Can I get you a drink?" he asks. "Not much of a selection, I'm afraid, but I have scotch, gin, some blackberry cordial—" She reaches into her purse and takes something out. He frowns. Not a gun, exactly, but it does seem like a weapon of some sort, a little glittering metal device that fits neatly in her hand. "Hey," he says, "what's—" "I'm so terribly sorry, Martin," she whispers, and a bolt of terrible fire slams into his chest.

She sips the drink. It relaxes her. The glass isn't very clean, but she isn't worried about picking up a disease, not after all the injections Friesling gave her. Martin looks as if he can stand some relaxing too. "Aren't you drinking?" she asks. "I suppose I will," he says. He pours himself some gin. She comes up behind him and slips her hand into the front of his bathrobe. His body is cool, smooth, hard. "Oh, Martin," she murmurs. "Oh! Martin!"

Ted takes a room in one of the commercial hotels downtown. The first thing he does is try to put a call through to Alice's mother in Chillicothe. He still isn't really convinced that his little time-jaunt flirtation has retroactively eliminated Alice from existence. But the call convinces him, all right. The middle-aged woman who answers is definitely not Alice's mother. Right phone number, right address—he badgers her for the information—but wrong woman. "You don't have a daughter named Alice Porter?" he asks three or four times. "You don't know anyone in the neighborhood who does? It's important." All right. Cancel the old lady, ergo cancel Alice. But now he has a different problem. How much of the universe has he altered by removing Alice and her mother? Does he live in some other city, now, and hold some other job? What has happened to Bobby and Tink? Frantically he begins phoning people. Friends, fellow workers, the man at the bank. The same response from all of them: blank stares, shakings of the head. We don't know you, fellow. He looks at himself in the mirror. Okay, he asks himself. Who am I?

Martin moves swiftly and purposefully, the way they taught him to do in the army when it's necessary to disarm a dangerous opponent. He lunges forward and catches the girl's arm, pushing it upward before she can fire the shiny whatzis she's aiming at him. She turns out to be stronger than he anticipated, and they struggle fiercely for the weapon. Suddenly it fires. Something like a lightning bolt explodes between them and knocks him to the floor, stunned. When he picks himself up, he sees her lying near the door with a charred hole in her throat.

The telephone's jangling clatter brings Martin up out of a dream in which he is ravishing Alice's luscious young body. Dry-throated, gummy-eyed, he reaches a palsied hand toward the receiver. "Yes?" he says. Ted's face blossoms on the screen. "Grandfather!" he blurts. "Are you all right?" "Of course I'm all right," Martin says testily. "Can't you tell? What's the matter with you, boy?" Ted shakes his head. "I don't know," he mutters. "Maybe it was only a bad dream. I imagined that Alice rented one of those time machines and went back to 1947. And tried to kill you so that I wouldn't ever have existed." Martin snorts. "What idiotic nonsense! How can she have killed me in 1947 when I'm here alive in 2006?"

Naked, Alice sinks into Martin's arms. His strong hands sweep eagerly over her breasts and shoulders and his mouth descends to hers. She shivers with desire. "Yes," she murmurs tenderly, pressing herself against him. "Oh, yes, yes, yes!" They'll do it and it'll be fantastic. And afterward she'll kill him with the kitchen carver while he's lying there savoring the event. But a troublesome thought occurs. If Martin dies in 1947, Ted doesn't get to be born in 1968. Okay. But what about Tink and Bobby? They won't get born either, not if I don't marry Ted. I'll be married to someone else when I get back to 2006, and I suppose I'll have different children. Bobby? Tink? What am I doing to you? Sudden fear congeals her, and she pulls back from the vigorous young man nuzzling her throat. "Wait," she says. "Listen, I'm sorry. It's all a big mistake. I'm sorry, but I've got to get out of here right away!"

So this is the year 1947. Well, well, well. Everything looks so cluttered and grimy and ancient. He hurries through the chilly streets toward his grandfather's place. If his luck is good and if Friesling's technicians have calculated things accurately, he'll be able to head Alice off. That might even be her now, that slender woman walking briskly half a block ahead of him. He steps up his pace. Yes, it's Alice, on her way to Martin's. Well done, Friesling! Ted approaches her warily, suspecting that she's armed. If she's capable of coming back to 1947 to kill Martin, she'd kill him just as readily. Especially back here where neither one of them has any legal existence. When he's close to her he says in a low, hard, intense voice, "Don't turn around, Alice. Just keep walking as if everything's perfectly normal." She stiffens. "Ted?" she cries, astonished. "Is that you, Ted?" "Damned right it is." He laughs harshly. "Come on. Walk to the corner and turn to your left around the block. You're going back to your machine and you're going to get the hell out of the twentieth century without harming anybody. I know what you were trying to do, Alice. But I caught you in time, didn't I?"

Martin is just getting down to real business when the door of his apartment bursts open and a man rushes in. He's middle-aged, stocky, with weird clothes—the ultimate in zoot suits, a maze of vividly contrasting colors and conflicting patterns, shoulders padded to resemble shelves—and a wild look in his eyes. Alice leaps up from the bed. "Ted!" she screams. "My God, what are you doing here?" "You murderous bitch," the intruder yells. Martin, naked and feeling vulnerable, his nervous system stunned by the interruption, looks on in amazement as the stranger grabs her and begins throttling her. "Bitch! Bitch! Bitch!" he roars, shaking her in a mad frenzy. The girl's face is turning black. Her eyes are bugging. After a long moment Martin breaks finally from his freeze. He stumbles forward, seizes the man's fingers, peels them away from the girl's throat. Too late. She falls limply and lies motionless. "Alice!" the intruder moans. "Alice, Alice, what have I done?" He drops to his knees beside her body, sobbing. Martin blinks. "You killed her," he says, not believing that any of this can really be happening. "You actually killed her!"

Alice's face appears on the telephone screen. Christ, how beautiful she is, Martin thinks, and his decrepit body quivers with lust. "There you are," he says. "I've been trying to reach you for hours. I had such a strange dream—that something awful had happened to Ted—and then your phone didn't answer, and I began to think maybe the dream was a premonition of some kind, an omen, you know—" Alice looks puzzled. "I'm afraid you have the wrong number, sir," she says sweetly, and hangs up.

She draws the laser, and the naked man cowers back against the wall in bewilderment. "What the hell is this?" he asks, trembling. "Put that thing down, lady. You've got the wrong guy." "No," she says. "You're the one I'm after. I hate to do this to you, Martin, but I've got no choice. You have to die." "Why?" he demands. *"Why?"* "You wouldn't understand it even if I told you," she says. She moves her finger toward the discharge stud. Abruptly there is a frightening sound of cracking wood and collapsing plaster behind her, as though an earthquake has struck. She whirls and is appalled to see her husband breaking down the door of Martin's apartment. "I'm just in time!" Ted exclaims. "Don't move, Alice!" He reaches for her. In panic she fires without thinking. The dazzling beam catches Ted in the pit of the stomach and he goes down, gurgling in agony, clutching at his belly as he dies.

The door falls with a crash, and this character in peculiar clothing materializes in a cloud of debris, looking crazier than Napoleon. It's incredible, Martin thinks. First an unknown broad rings his bell and invites herself in and takes her clothes off, and then, just as he's about to screw her, this happens. It's pure Marx Brothers, only dirty. But Martin's not going to take any crap. He pulls himself away from the panting, gasping girl on the bed, crosses the room in three quick strides, and seizes the newcomer. "Who the hell are you?" Martin demands, slamming him hard against the wall. The girl is dancing around behind him. "Don't hurt him!" she wails. "Oh, please, don't hurt him!"

Ted certainly hadn't expected to find them in bed together. He understood why she might have wanted to go back in time to murder Martin, but simply to have an affair with him—no, it didn't make sense. Of course, it was altogether likely that she had come here to kill and had paused for a little dalliance first. You never could tell about women, even your own wife. Alley cats, all of them. Well, a lucky thing for him that she had given him these few extra minutes to get here. "Okay," he says. "Get your clothes on, Alice. You're coming with me." "Just a second, mister," Martin growls. "You've got your goddamned nerve, busting in like this." Ted tries to explain, but the words won't come. It's all too complicated. He gestures mutely at Alice, at himself, at Martin. The next moment Martin jumps him and they go tumbling together to the floor.

"Who are you?" Martin yells, banging the intruder repeatedly against the wall. "You some kind of detective? You trying to work a badger game on me?" Slam. Slam. Slam. He feels the girl's small fists pounding on his own back. "Stop it!" she screams. "Let him alone, will you? He's my husband!" *"Husband!"* Martin cries. Astounded, he lets go of the stranger and swings around to face the girl. A moment later he realizes his mistake. Out of the corner of his eye he sees that the intruder has raised his fists high above his head like clubs. Martin tries to get out of the way, but no time, no time, and the fists descend with awful force against his skull.

Alice doesn't know what to do. They're rolling around on the floor, fighting like wildcats, now Martin on top, now Ted. Martin is younger and bigger and stronger, but Ted seems possessed by the strength of the insane; he's gone berserk. Both men are bloody-faced and furniture is crashing over everywhere. Her first impulse is to get between them and stop this crazy fight somehow. But then she remembers that she has come here as a killer, not as a peacemaker. She gets the laser from her purse and aims it at Martin, but then the combatants do a flip-flop and it is Ted who is in the line of fire. She hesitates. It doesn't matter which one she shoots, she realizes after a moment. They both have to die, one way or another. She takes aim. Maybe she can get them both with one bolt. But as her finger starts to tighten on the discharge stud Martin suddenly gets Ted in a bear hug and, half lifting him, throws him five feet across the room. The back of Ted's neck hits the wall and there is a loud *crack*. Ted slumps and is still. Martin gets shakily to his feet. "I think I killed him," he says. "Christ, who the hell was he?" "He was your grandson," Alice says, and begins to shriek hysterically.

Ted stares in horror at the crumpled body at his feet. His hands still tingle from the impact. The left side of Martin's head looks as though a pile driver has crushed it. "Good God in heaven," Ted says thickly, "what have I done? I came here to protect him and I've killed him! I've killed my own grandfather!" Alice, wide-eyed, futilely trying to cover her nakedness by folding one arm across her breasts and spreading her other hand over her loins, says, "If he's dead, why are you still here? Shouldn't you have disappeared?" Ted shrugs. "Maybe I'm safe as long as I remain here in the past. But the moment I try to go back to 2006, I'll vanish as though I've never been. I don't know. I don't understand any of this. What do you think?"

Alice steps uncertainly from the machine into the Temponautics showroom. There's Friesling. There are the technicians. Friesling says, smiling, "I hope you had a very enjoyable journey, Mrs. . . . ah . . . uh . . ." He falters. "I'm sorry," he says, reddening, "but your name seems to have escaped me." Alice says, "It's . . . ah . . . Alice . . . uh . . . do you know, the second name escapes me too?"

The whole clan has gathered to celebrate Martin's eighty-third birthday. He cuts the cake, and then one by one they go to him to kiss him. When it's Alice's turn, he deftly spins her around so that he screens her from the others, and gives her rump a good hearty pinch. "Oh, if I were only fifty years younger!" he sighs.

It's a warm springlike day. Everything has been lovely at the office—three new accounts all at once—and the trip home on the freeway was a breeze. Alice is waiting for him, dressed in her finest and sexiest outfit, all ready to go out. It's a special day. Their eleventh anniversary. How beautiful she looks! He kisses her, she kisses him, he takes the tickets from his pocket with a grand flourish. "Surprise," he says. "Two weeks in Hawaii, starting next Tuesday! Happy anniversary!" "Oh, Ted!" she cries. "How marvelous! I love you, Ted darling!" He pulls her close to him again. "I love you, Alice dear."

RANDY-TANDY MAN

by Ross Rocklynne

Ross Rocklynne has been writing science fiction since the mid-1930's, and his early stories bore such titles as "Trans-Plutonian Trap," "Slaves of the Ninth Moon," and "The Reflection That Lived." Times change and so does science fiction; today we prefer stories that rely less on melodrama. Yet Rocklynne remains a familiar name on science-fiction contents pages; he has a lively, original mind, and his ideas continue to be stimulating. Maybe it's because, as he shows in this delightful story, he still retains all his enthusiasm for the future.

THE RANDY-TANDY man's coming, Kerbisher yells to himself, exuberant. This Free Term is for the birds. Who's scared of the Randy-Tandy man?

Skipping, hollering, and happy—this is Kerbisher, big oaf in an oafish world. He's worked his three hours today, and that's it; he's anything but tired, so he has the rest of the day to be relaxed, joyous, and TV'd.

"Honey, I'm home," he yells, kicking off his shoes, heavy with the dirt of wrecked buildings, and peeling off his work shirt, which he drops into a slot along with other countless shirts belonging to other oafs in an overpopulated world. "I'm home," he repeats, "and I'm going to stay home, and revel in love, liberty, and understanding. Come Monday, the Randy-Tandy man!"

The wife comes in from the kitchen, little, smiling as always, and polishing a spoon and a knife with a piece of marvel cloth. "Then Monday's the day, if you say so," she says, smiling, "but you could be wrong, it just might be today. Whichever, a little hate isn't going to kill you, honey, you got to remember that, so why be scared of the Randy-Tandy man?"

Kerbisher grabs her, kissing her nicely. "Mmm-mmmm," he says, "this happy stuff poops me out, did you know that? I got a book somewhere."

Kerbisher, a man of many moods, changing, and changeable. His delightful wife has returned to the kitchen, where she is baking a potato or two and a half-steak made of crushed almonds. He is stretched out, enjoying his life and reading his book. This Kerbisher—literary, erudite; or at least as literary and erudite as it is necessary to be in the day of the Great Generation that's going to make everybody great. So . . . just look at the ray-gun tanning the scaly hide off that Ganymedan!

Ring-a-ling! That's the muted telephone. "Mr. Kerbisher? This is the R&D and T&D representative in your community. A new day is dawning. Hearken well."

"I'm hearkening," yells Kerbisher, while he thinks, with a surprised shiver, Emily is right: the Randy-Tandy man comes today, Saturday, not Monday. How come she made that good guess about the Randy-Tandy man?

"Big ears, Mr. Kerbisher," says the Randy-Tandy man, pleasant and cool as always. Oh, those polite Randy-Tandy men have it all figured out: come someday, what a world we're going to have.

"Big ears," repeats the Randy-Tandy man in his silky soft, apologetic, but firm voice. "You understand what is being said, Mr. Kerbisher?"

"Do I understand?" yells Kerbisher, so enthusiastically his wife Emily runs in from the kitchen with a wondering smile on her face. "You're telling me it's the end of the Free Term, Mr. Randy-Tandy man," he cries, hugging his picture book. "Now we've got to hate!"

"Exactly, Mr. Kerbisher. Hate people with big ears. You've got it straight, now?"

"I do, I do. Hate people with—" Kerbisher's voice fails. He is watching Emily standing in the doorway of the kitchen. Little wife has big ears! Moreover, her hair is caught up around her head with clips so that her ears stand out more than usual. One could hardly miss the fact that her ears are big. Kerbisher's great jaw trembles.

"—Big," he says, faltering.

"Don't say it out loud," shushes the Randy-Tandy man. "As you know, everybody will hate something different. Your specific prejudice is big ears. You understand, sir?"

"Yes," says Kerbisher, almost weeping.

"Very good."

"How long will the Revile and Despise Term last?"

"Three days, sir. Then the Taper Off and Deny Period, to

last as long as your discretion seems to dictate. You understand, sir?"

"I do," sobs Kerbisher.

The hate begins. Kerbisher puts the phone down slowly.
How many times since high school began has he fumbled the
phone into the slot after getting his instructions from the
Randy-Tandy man? Maybe a few hundred times, but never
slowly like this. Oh, already big Kerbisher is suffering.

"Who was it?" asks his wife Emily, coming up behind him
and rapidly dusting a jug. "The Randy-Tandy man, I dare say.
A little early, maybe? On Saturday after all?"

"Yes, that's right," says Kerbisher, looking away. He is feeling it again, the feeling he must feel if man and his works are
to survive. The hate made to order, like always. Oh, Emily,
Emily, his black thoughts run, our time has come. Now we
must part. Our intertwined lives—well, it's just as if he's
TV'ing.

Sweet Emily, dusting rapidly, comes up behind him like a
cyclone. He shakes her off and cries thickly, "I'm going out,
Emily, I can't stay here." Putting on a clean shirt, flailing out
his arms.

"Dinner?" she says. "You aren't going to be here for dinner? Two potatoes and a healthy half-steak? Walter—"

He swears, whirling on her. "Haven't I told you, no half-
steak? Haven't I? Haven't I?"

"Well, not in just so many words. Not just exactly that way.
You said—"

"How many times have I told you? How many times? No
half-steak!"

The little woman, she stands there, looking, her hair lifted
back from big ears, and she just stands there, not even smiling, and that's when Kerbisher oafishly goes. He's out the
door like a shot, breathing hard and running, and remembering it all over again like when he was a smart kid twenty years
ago.

Smart, yes, but the Randy-Tandy man was smarter. The

Randy-Tandy man came to the school then, and he talked to all the kids in the auditorium.

"All you short boys," he says, that time twenty years ago, "you're going to hate the tall boys, right?"

The short boys, back then, they just sit there; they don't say anything. The Randy-Tandy man says, "Come, come, don't you know how to hate? Haven't you always had a tiny, sneaking hate for all those tall boys? Of course you have. But now you must hate a little harder, on purpose. Those are the rules we're going to follow from now on. Do not be difficult.

"Very well, let's hear it from the tall boys. You'll find it easy enough to hate those inferior short boys, won't you?"

The tall boys, they laugh and jog each other in the ribs. "Listen to that R&D man," they yell. "We don't hate the little squirts. Not much. Do we have to?"

"It's the new rules," says the Randy-Tandy man firmly.

The tall boys giggle and yell, "Might as well be them shorties, Mr. R&D man, if we got to hate somebody!"

The Randy-Tandy man nods approvingly. "And the shorties are going to hate you back just as hard.

"I'll give you," he goes on, "three days for the Revile and Despise Period, all you boys, not the girls—they can hate each other next week. I want you to work at the hate for three days. Those are the rules. Then Taper Off and Deny for two days or so, and after that we'll have an easy Free Term until the next hate."

Well, all that three days the shorties and the tall boys mix it up with each other, with the girls looking on and giggling. At first, they walk circles around one another. They look at one another out of the corners of their eyes, their heads bent angle-wise, the shorties looking up and the tall guys looking down.

"Hey there, shorties," comes a giggle from a tall guy. "Okay, big shit, just watch it," says a shortie. And he means it. Randy-Tandy man says he has to mean it.

The shorties and the tall guys do circles around each other.

Then the fights begin. The principal and the teachers and the school custodians are in there breaking up the fights. Then they begin again. And it isn't only the fighting, it's the Reviling and the Despising, the insults, and the swearing.

Then the three days of the Revile and Despise end. It is hard, it is mighty hard, to cut off the hate. But sure enough, on the third day the tall guys and the shorties somehow begin Tapering Off. Oh, a little fight or punishing word now and then, but they all end up laughing about it, and shaking hands, and hugging each other, and swinging off to class with arms around one another's shoulders, and first thing you know—yes, Kerbisher among them!—they're Denying! "I didn't mean it, shortie, you got a punch just like you were tall." "I didn't mean your brains was skinny, too, tall boy." So they're into the Free Term!

The Free Terms are a relief, of course—for a while, anyway. You don't have to go around hating anybody unless you want to. But in the middle of the Free Term, usually, the tension begins to grow. You feel the Randy-Tandy man is about to come again, and you're excited about it, and hating it and liking it at the same time, and you're finally glad when the suspense is over.

"Now, boys and girls," the Randy-Tandy man might say, his eyes darting from here to there around the auditorium, "we're going to try a little blond-brunette thing this week. Any of you blond boys or girls like to stand up and spout a little brunette hate for a starter? Then we'll have an R&D of, say, two days, followed by the usual T&D, and then the usual Free Term."

Well, that's the way it is, all through grade school and junior high. The Randy-Tandy man tells you what to hate about people, and you don't ask why, because the Randy-Tandy man knows what he's doing. You hate people and get hated back. Then you Taper Off and Deny, and end up so relieved you love everybody through the Free Term.

Oh, those Free Terms! Honestly, you could jump the school wall. It doesn't matter if you've got freckles or pigeon-toes or crow's-feet, crooked teeth or pretty teeth or teeth with braces on them; if you're bowlegged or you lisp; if you're modest, shy, or pushy, fat or thin, poor or rich, black or white, Mex or Chink, or any one of a *million* things! You don't have to worry about getting picked on during the Free Term.

Come the end of the Free Term, though, watch out! Because there's the shivery old Randy-Tandy man standing on the stage looking you over.

"Well, boys and girls," he might say, "what'll it be this time? How about a good solid hate from all you smart intellectuals who dig good grammar? Sort of despise the kids who can't parse a sentence, right?"

Or "All you girls with good manners, how'd you like to take it out on those rough boys who don't know the score when it comes to treating you sweet young things just right? Get in there, girls. Really hate. For about three days. That'll show 'em! Of course, they won't find it too hard to hate you right back."

A grand, shivery, exciting time of life that never lets up—this Kerbisher remembers.

Everybody's got something wrong with him, and everybody likes to do a little hating now and then, so any time you want to hate something about somebody, you just wait for the Randy-Tandy man to bring it out. He'll be along with the proper hate in due course, and he doesn't care if you use him.

For instance, there's Kerbisher's bad grades one semester. He has to blame them on somebody; after all, it can't be Kerbisher's fault. So he picks on this blue-eyed, giggling girl sitting behind him all semester. He blows up, using junior high swearwords you wouldn't put in a book. After all, how can he study when she's giggling? Anyway, this is the week he's supposed to hate giggling girls, preferably pretty ones

with blue eyes. And you can't expect her just to sit there—
not, anyway, when this is the week she has a prejudice
against big-nosed boys like Kerbisher. Whop! She hits him
across the nose with her psychology book. Well, you can
imagine what happens during the T&D! Quite the reverse,
which makes everything seem worthwhile in a funny way.

Then junior high is over, and Kerbisher is floating high in
a summer haze which he hopes will not end. The Randy-
Tandy man is the source of Kerbisher's worry. What's the
Randy-Tandy man thinking about? Will he follow Kerbisher
into high school? What kind of badness is he planning? *Ring-
a-ling!* That's the way it comes about, the Randy-Tandy man
calling up high school kids and plaguing them again—right
in their own homes!

"Hello there, Mr. Kerbisher. A new day dawns. Got a four-
day Revile and Despise coming up, son, calculated for you
especially, under our Advanced Plan. Anybody who reads
books. Got that, son?"

"Got it!" yells the young oaf Kerbisher, making out like
he's happy that summer-long Free Term is over. "But I read
myself. A lot. Comics."

"Books, son, not comics. Anybody that studies, or tries to
advance himself through study. Hate them eggheads, boy!"

Kerbisher is alone with his hates, under the Advanced
Plan. He's not allowed to tell anybody what he might be
hating. Therefore, he never knows for sure what somebody
might be hating about him. How can Kerbisher, or anybody,
live like this? Everybody does. Everybody, so far as Kerbisher knows, is in the same fix he's in, so he pads through the
jungle of hate and bigotry, and with his cat eyes and sense of
smell he learns to sense what is going on in the little hating
minds around him.

For instance, this oaf Kerbisher knows for a fact that he's
been hated and sneered at and Reviled and Despised because 1) he's dumb, 2) he's smart, 3) he goes with girls, 4) he

doesn't go with girls, and finally, in his senior year, 5) he's in love, and 6) going to get married.

Love? Marriage? How in the world does Kerbisher manage marriage in the middle of all this hate that the Randy-Tandy man is bringing to the world? It's a miracle, folks, so step right up and view the events which lead to the fairly happy married life of little Emily Draper and Walter Kerbisher. Kerbisher's already gone through a girl-hating R&D, years ago, and Emily, so small and low-breasted she seems lost in Kerbisher's shadow, is a delight, and she doesn't do anything but keep house, not even read. It so happens that in all the eight months they go together, meeting first at the Methodist Church, they only have one R&D, and that's her hating him.

Oh, but she gives it to him good! For two days she is so vilely upset by Kerbisher that he gives her cramps.

"You give me cramps!" the sweet girl, gone crazy because of the Randy-Tandy man, screams at him. "You walk so heavy you make my cake fall, and dirty up the floor besides! If you want to marry me, you got to walk light!"

Kerbisher, falling terribly in love with little Emily Draper, is beside himself. Certainly he wants to marry her, and you can bet he stops walking heavy right then, or at least until the R&D ends, and they get into the T&D. After that, things sail. Married two years, folks, and the real miracle is, after this, never once does Emily seem to get into an R&D. Imagine that. Emily is the perfect wife, treats her husband to outstanding meals, smiles a lot, loves him nicely, and tries to help him when the Randy-Tandy man puts him in a state. But no Reviling and Despising from Emily, from then on.

Here's Kerbisher, fretting, angry, hating, cursing, Reviling and Despising, big oaf in an oafish world, and his wife Emily never gets into an R&D. Why, just about all she does is smile.

"Oh," answers Emily to this, while she polishes a fork and a knife with a piece of marvel cloth, "I dare say ever'body gets into an R&D now and then, with or without the Randy-

Tandy man. I've been in some turrible frets, Walter, turrible!

"As for the smiling, maybe we'll all be smiling one of these days, Walter—if not outside, then inside." She smiles while polishing two glass bowls and a plate.

The Smiling People, Emily among them, hang on the edge of your mind, just out of sight—smiling and happy and never getting upset! It's enough to worry Kerbisher half to death. Everybody has to go through these hate spasms, don't they? And then they have to go through times of love and happiness after that, don't they? Isn't that the way things are? So it must be imaginary, this feeling that smiling, happy people are all around you.

Is it imaginary, though, seeing his wife Emily smiling, with her hair clipped up on her head so that her big ears stand out? It's almost as if she knew the hateful Randy-Tandy man was going to instruct Kerbisher to hate big ears.

It's no wonder that oaf Kerbisher runs. He's gone, down the street, a wild man, his comic book dropped on the floor at her feet, and there he goes.

Down the street he goes, howling and flailing his arms, and virtually everybody he sees seems to have big ears. He's fleeing past Bill Stotter's place, and Bill Stotter waves from his porch, smiling up a storm of good will, and nodding his head so his big ears seem to dip a little.

Kerbisher is in such a state with the vileness of hate the Randy-Tandy man brought him that he shakes his fist at Bill Stotter and shouts obscenities. Bill Stotter only smiles, and waves big ears. This makes matters worse for poor Kerbisher. Bill Stotter is one of the Smiling People! Why does he always smile?

Kerbisher rushes down the street.

Why does it have to be like this?

He returns home, where he sits, trembling. He does not want to see his wife Emily, and she does not try to see him. He sneaks into the kitchen at night. Once he sneaks in during the day, to get the remains of his nighttime sandwich, and there is Emily, polishing a red apple which she is making plans to eat.

Kerbisher is beside himself. He shakes his fists, shouting, "Now I know it isn't the ears at all, it's the way your hair is up!"

"My hair is up," she says. "Oh. Well."

"But it isn't that at all!"

"Well, I dare say it has to be something," says she, working on the red apple.

"It's the smile!" cries Kerbisher.

"I do smile at times, Walter. You may have hit on something there."

"And it's because you never get into an R&D," he cries, his face puffing up redly at the despicable thought. "I'm beginning to understand what this is all about, woman!"

"I dare say it's about time," she observes, propping herself on a tall chair, and studying herself in the polished red apple.

Kerbisher waves both fists. "It isn't fair," he cries. "We've got our rules in this world. It's the only road to the Great Generation. We must learn to hate, hate, hate, and then Taper Off with love, love, love.

"But you don't go by the rules!" he yells at the eating Emily. "You don't pay any attention to the Randy-Tandy man. He calls, you say phooey. Tell me you don't do it that way, just tell me."

"Well," she says, having some trouble talking around a mouthful of apple.

Kerbisher throws up his hands. He is red and perspiring. How can he say such things? Oh, Emily, Emily, he whimpers inside himself as if he's TV'ing again. He blunders toward his room, and never comes out again until the Revile and Despise period is over. He wakes in the morning and the Tapering Off and Denying period has begun. He finds Emily in the kitchen working over dishes.

"Uch-hmm," Kerbisher coughs.

"Yes, dear."

"You do smile a lot, and you do seem to have big ears, although not as big as one would suppose," he tells her.

"I would be the last to deny it," says Emily, swiping with a dishcloth at a shining tumbler.

"But smiling isn't a bad thing, and you can hear nicely with big ears."

"I'm glad you've made the discovery," smiles Emily.

"Uch-hmm," coughs oaf Kerbisher, fleeing the scene. But he begins to leave his room, and on the second day of the Tapering Off, he returns to work. As he works, wrecking buildings, this Kerbisher, this big oaf, begins to smile. "Yahoo!" he is yelling inside, riding the bucking bronco of himself across the range under western skies. He's back to loving again.

Yahoo! He's into the house, tossing off his shirt, grabbing at Emily, and whirling her like a flag of joy. "Randy-Tandy man," he says grimly, and cries out some junior high school swearwords which he happens to remember.

Now Kerbisher finds that he is anxious to talk to the Randy-Tandy man. Where's the Randy-Tandy man? The Free Term goes on and on. Kerbisher frets, pacing the floor, and forgetting his comic book. What do you do to get hold of a Randy-Tandy man?

Kerbisher's sweet wife Emily muses, "But why? Why would you want to get hold of a Randy-Tandy man, of all people?"

"Because I'm going to tell him what's what," Kerbisher declares. "He drove me crazy this last time. I'm through with hating. Nothing but loving after this, Emily doll."

So it is that less than two hours later the Randy-Tandy man calls.

At the sound of all that smoothness of voice, Kerbisher almost crumbles. His resolve begins to fade. He has to grit his teeth to say what he has to say.

"I'm Mr. Kerbisher," he shoots back without too much delay. "Mr. Randy-Tandy man, you can stop right there. Don't say any more. It's all over. After this, the only prejudice I've got in this life is against the Randy-Tandy man."

"Indeed?" says the Randy-Tandy man. "Against the R&D and T&D man, of all people?"

"You heard me," says Kerbisher.

"But you don't seem excited. You don't seem angry. You don't seem to have built a proper foundation of hate."

"Because I'm in a long Free Term," says Kerbisher, with a strong sound in his voice. "This Free Term is going to last all my life. I'm not singing any more of your little hate songs. I'm not dancing any more of your bigot trots. I am a Free Man," he finishes, TV'ing it a little.

The Randy-Tandy man is silent.

"Well," he says, and his voice is all smiles.

Smiles!

Kerbisher almost drops through the floor. The Randy-Tandy man says warmly, "My personal congratulations, Mr. Kerbisher! We have been waiting for this moment. Your name will be entered in our Exempt Files. What this means is that you are officially exempt for life from the necessities of bigotry, prejudice, and/or hate. Good day, sir, and my congratulations again. It's been a rough battle for all of us. And all we had to do was to learn we didn't have to put up with it, right? And, oh yes, Mr. Kerbisher?"

"Huh?" says Kerbisher.

"I would like to inform you that one of our representatives will call on you this evening."

Kerbisher hangs up, and sees Emily smiling. "Emily," he says sternly, and that's when they have it out, but without any R&D, mind you.

In the evening, Bill Stotter, the Kerbishers' smiling neighbor from down the street, pays Kerbisher a visit, just as the Randy-Tandy man said he would. Well, you can just imagine being face-to-face with a Randy-Tandy man, who sticks out his hand, smiling, and shakes Kerbisher's hand, and says, "Mr. Kerbisher, I am the R&D and T&D representative you have an appointment with this evening. I am here to ask you a favor, to ensure the dawning of a new day throughout our world."

Oh, the Randy-Tandy man still visits the schools, still makes his calls. There is no other way; people have to learn they don't have to do it. Anyway, the next time the Randy-Tandy man calls somebody, he should listen carefully, because it just might be the voice of that big oaf Kerbisher!

THE WORLD IS A SPHERE

by Edgar Pangborn

Edgar Pangborn's stories of a post-holocaust North America have already been collected into one book, the fondly remembered Davy, *and there'll be another book before long. "Tiger Boy" in* Universe 2 *marked his return to this richly imagined world, and here's another: a coolly impassioned story of the enslavement of tomorrow's mutants . . . and tomorrow's minds.*

"WE HAVE slain bigger monsters," said Ian Moltas, Deliberator of the Ninth Ward of Norlenas. He had spoken aloud within his solitude; the words brought him no consolation, no increase of courage. After a while a man, or a people, will grow weary of slaying monsters, and then back comes the rule of disorder.

He stood by a western window of his museum in the tropic night, his hands pleased by the cool stone sill, his ears accepting the innocent clamor of the dark—insect shrilling, intermittent husky roar of a rutting alligator in the swamp at the border of his parkland, and now and then the trill and chuckle of the nitingal, bird of mystery. They tell us it's good luck to hear that on a clear night of the old moon.

No one ever sees the nitingal, yet it lived in the world at least two hundred years ago in the great time of the Republic, for the poets of that age spoke of it, and by that singing name.

Good luck? Ian Moltas no longer believed in luck of either sort. Out of confusions, sufferings, compromises, you won what you could: let God and the Devil contend for the rest.

"We have cut down monsters like you before," he said, and held up a clotted fist, shutting away the twinkle of lamps in the palace windows half a mile off across the parkland. He did not let his fist obscure the tender brilliance of the old moon declining. Under those lamps the Emperor's clerks might carry the day's toil to midnight or beyond—Musons all, of course, and therefore slaves dependent for life itself on the Emperor's whim. Dwarfish, with delicate hands, high foreheads, often that telltale sixth finger, the poor devils would scratch away at their mean tasks—recording, copying documents and correspondence, above all transcribing to fine vellum the latest imperial rantings and platitudes in the service of Emperor Asta's immortality; and no one would guess from the small pale Muson faces what fires might be ablaze behind their masks. Moltas supposed he knew a little about that; he was not arrogant enough to think that he, a Misipan of the ruling class, could know very much. To know anything at all of it might be regarded as treason to his peers.

The Emperor Asta was already officially a god by act of the Assembly of Deliberators (Moltas concurring—what can one do?), but he would not rest content with that. Two of the three preceding emperors had also been deified, so the bloom was off that peach. No—he meant to be known to eternity as a great thinker, statesman, and literary artist. Unfortunately, he had never had an original idea, and could barely read and write.

"We'll cut you down too." But Moltas, listening for the iron ring of rebellion in his voice, did not hear it. Can you have rebellion without the people? Can rebellion speak in elderly tones with a quaver, almost a note of peevishness? After all, the quarrel was not between him, Deliberator of the Ninth Ward, and the gaunt little egomaniac over there in the palace; it was between the spark of evil in the human world and the spark of good. As for the people—

The Republic! Ah, they said, *the Republic! Yes, we must bring back the Republic, but not just now, because the Emperor (long live the Emperor) has promised to do it himself the first moment it seems practical. Bread and rice! More fights! More fuck-shows in the Stadium! Long live the Emperor! Fights! Fuck-shows! BREAD AND RICE!*

And the Assembly of Deliberators, once the very heart and conscience of the Republic? Moltas thought: *Why, we are mostly old men, and the waves have gone over us. The Republic is not to be brought back only by remembering it with tears.*

The stone sill was paining his hands. He rubbed his fingers and straightened his elderly back, and turned to the spacious quiet of the room he called his museum—like all the house, a little too grand and a little shabby. The spoils of a rich man's curiosity had accumulated here for thirty years. Not wanting to trouble a servant for such a trifle, he touched a taper to a bracket-lamp and carried the flame to a standing lamp on a long table in the center of the room. The table was of mahogany, careful Misipan workmanship of about a hundred and fifty years ago, from the last years of the Republic; but one would not think of it as old compared to the dozen treasures that stood on it, most of them from the American age, the Age of Sorcerers.

Oldest of all, he thought, was a crude two-faced image of blackened stonelike substance, probably clay, male on one side, female on the other, which surely belonged to some period earlier than the Age of Sorcerers, although the mere notion was heresy. A few years ago he had noticed the image in the trashy wares of a peddler from the north, who let it go for one menin, almost a junk price. It really had nothing in common with American relics. However . . .

Time was not, said the priests, until Sol-Amra made the world out of water and air and earth and fire, and gave it to the Americans, the Sorcerers, who became afflicted with the sin of pride, and were destroyed by pestilence and fire, all but a handful. And we, the remote descendants of that handful, are still corrupt, and must continue to bear the divine curses of poverty and mutation until the year 7000, when Sol-Amra comes to judge the world. Poverty is punishment for the sin of greed. Mutation is punishment for our lecherous nature. Most corrupt of all are the Musons, for does not the wrath of God show clearly in their dwarfish size, pallid faces, evil hands? So let them be safely held in slavery, and sacrificed at the Spring Festivals to take upon them the sin of the world.

One knew all that, and knew the necessity of ritual agreement. One also belonged to the not-quite-secret society of the Tera, discreetly smiling in private at the barbarity of the times; even smiling, very privately and rather dangerously, at Sol-Amra and the Lesser Pantheon. These traditions and legends, you know, said the gentlemen of the Tera—excellent stuff for the multitude. Must have something to keep them happy, while we pursue philosophy and pure reason and the quiet life.

If any visitor showed interest in the two-faced image, Ian Moltas would shrug and dismiss it as a curiosity of no importance, most likely made by the little naked savages in that wilderness away up north, west of Penn; or it might even have come from the scarcely explored lake country much farther north. But Moltas had seen enough of the barbarous wooden images and clumsy pottery of those savages to know that this two-faced image was nothing of theirs.

The other treasures on the table were relics of the American age, valuable but not unfamiliar to connoisseurs. A gray metal dish known to have come from the jungle-buried ruins east of Nathes (apparently called Natchez in the Age of Sorcerers, with heaven knows what pronunciation). A tiny cylinder of an unknown bright metal tapered to a hollow point, with part of an inscription still visible, a few of the antique letters that so closely resemble the Misipan alphabet. A disk of heavy glass with the mystic power of magnification. A tray of coins, some of corroded copper, others that appeared untouched by age.

Ian Moltas slumped in one of the massive chairs by the table. At the uncommon age of fifty-eight he was heavy but not fat, not very wrinkled, only somewhat gray. Mild sea-blue eyes belied the fierceness of his beaky nose; his flexible orator's mouth was darkly bracketed. He was wearing the scarlet loincloth of the ruling class; his sleeveless white tunic carried on the front the gold-and-green rice-plant symbol of the Assembly of Deliberators. Often if angry or depressed he sought for quiet in the contemplation of the clay image, and often found it. It must have been made, he thought, by fingers alone. How simple the gouges that marked the eyes! The mouths had been achieved by pressure of a thumbnail gone back to dust how many hundreds or thousands of years ago?

He looked up, startled and vague. "Yes, Elkan?" The slave had come silently, or might have been standing in the shadows several moments. He was trained, of course, to go about like a ghost, to be present suddenly whenever needed; but that magical quiet was also a part of the Muson nature.

"A peddler, Deliberator—perhaps not worth your time, but he was insistent. He gives his name as Piet Brun. He apologized for the late hour, saying he didn't wish to carry his treasure in the streets by daylight. This seemed irrational to me—whatever he has is carried in an ordinary sack—and I said so. He replied, with a smile—a rather unpleasant smile, sir, or so I thought—that he felt stronger than others in the dark. I did not like him, Deliberator, but I told him I would bring in his name."

"Does he say what he has?"

"No, sir, only that he thinks you might want to buy it. He says he was Misipan born but has spent most of his time traveling and trading in the barbarous northern countries. His speech suggests it—trader's jargon, quite coarse."

"Well, I'll see him. These people often do have something. But let him wait a few moments—I want to talk to you." Elkan also waited, quiet as the clay image. He was tall for a Muson, nearly five feet, which modified the deceptive child-like proportions that most of them had because of their large heads and stocky bodies, and he was eighty years old, middle-aged for his breed. He stood with arms folded—they never lost an alertness that seemed to cost them no effort—and his pale six-fingered hands spread out over the elbows as if to emphasize their difference. "Elkan, you'll remember that two years ago, two full years, I introduced a measure in the Assembly which would have declared that your people, sharing a common ancestry with humankind, a common language, a history of coexistence—"

" '—are and of right ought to be equal with the human race before the law and in every aspect of our social being.' Forgive the interruption, Deliberator. The words—your own, I believe—have sung in my mind a long time." Elkan's eyes, large and luminous, now and then met Moltas' gaze like the touch of a roving beam of light. "The measure, I presume, has been defeated, sir?"

"Oh, the measure—no, not exactly, not formally. Many times debated, cut to pieces and cobbled together again, saved up in committee for further waste of words, but never quite defeated. I had no hope at any time—as I think I told you—of winning all or even most of what we prayed for. I did hope that by asking for all we might win something. If we had merely won that technical admission of equality, it would have become impossible, by any kind of logic, for the law to say, as it does now, that your people are to exist forever in a state of slavery. The Assembly was almost ready for that simple first step at the time of Asta's accession. No, Elkan, the measure has not been defeated, but— Oh my God, how am I to tell you? . . . Elkan, the best hope of your people was always the Assembly. Nothing good can be expected from any other political source. We Deliberators—we are all that remains of a Republic that once did uphold an ideal of virtue, limited though it was; and it's on my mind tonight that we are not much. And I am obliged to tell you—you must know it for your own safety—the Assembly itself may be dying."

"There have always been passages of failing light." The Muson way, to state anything important as neutrally as possible, not in denial of passion—far from it—but in order to protect rational discourse from the tumults of the heart.

"Elkan, I have allowed myself to think that in talking to you—whom I have come to love as a friend, if I may say it —I am talking to others who cannot hear me directly. I do not want to learn anything about any groups of your people who may be living somehow in the wilderness, because like anyone I might become weak and betray you if my mind disintegrated under torture. However, if any such groups exist I wish them to hear this warning: be more careful than ever in the next few years while Asta lives. Do nothing to stir up the lust of violence. Asta is insecure. He needs a scape-goat, and your people would again be the victims, especially if the Assembly dies. He would not hold back from another Night of Knives—might welcome it."

Elkan said after a while, "The message will be transmitted, Deliberator. The advice may not be followed. Conditions change, my lord. The Night of Knives ten years ago was indecisive."

Moltas looked up, amazed at the overtones. Elkan's face was quiet as always. "Elkan, since the law forbids the freeing of Muson slaves under any conditions, I drew up a will which bequeaths you to my brother-in-law at Nathes. He is a kind soul, a scholar, and fortunate in that he knows almost nothing of the modern world, being concerned with the quarrels and delights of antiquity."

Elkan bowed. "An act of kindness, Deliberator." And it seemed to Moltas that the overtones were saying darkly and jubilantly: *If you die, my lord, I shall be with my people in the wilderness.*

"I'll see that peddler now."

Piet Brun stepped in with the brash grace of a tomcat, a small, bouncing man, gnarled and baldheaded, carrying a green cloth sack. Rudely he hitched a chair nearer the Deliberator's, waiting for no invitation to sit down. When Elkan brought in the second-best wine, Brun tossed off a glass as one swills water, clucked and patted his belly and said, "Very nice, sir. Much obliged." Behind Brun's back, Elkan shared Moltas' amusement with one lifted eyebrow, and faded from sight.

Casually Brun offered autobiography. He had been every-where and done everything. Born at Alsandra (he said), at thirteen he had run away to join a caravan bound for Penn in the barbarian north. He had served as a mercenary in one of Penn's border wars with the Empire of Katskil (a rising nation, he thought). After that he had a nice thing smuggling spearheads of Katskil steel to the savages in the lake country. He married, but his wife bore a mue, as they called such monstrosities up north, and then another, so he divorced her as Penn law permitted, an action that made her a protected slave of the Amran Church. At mention of that church, Brun automatically made the sign of the wheel over his heart, and scratched his armpit.

Repressing distaste, Moltas inquired, "You became a member of that church, Misur Brun, although Misipan born?"

Brun glanced around the room, maybe looking for eavesdroppers. "Got some nice things here, m'lord. Well, the church—see, I'm a *practical* man, Deliberator. I leave the thinking to the priests—they get paid for it." He laid a grubby finger along his nose, and winked. "Up north, you know, you're a follower of Abraham—I mean, what the church says is the faith of Abraham, or"—he slid the edge of his hand across his throat—"*ssst!*" He gulped more wine. "I had me a junk shop for a while—did all right but sold out. Itching foot, m'lord. Been a bit of a rascal maybe."

Moltas refilled his glass. The politician in him instinctively searched for nuggets of information. "You'd say that Katskil is the major power up north nowadays?"

"Not a doubt of it, sir. They ain't a naval power yet, but they aim to be that too. Country's riddled with witchcraft, by the way. Church does its best to keep it down, I give 'em credit for that." He glanced at the two-faced image and his eyes skittered away. "That lumin kettle there, that's a nice little piece, m'lord, right out of the Age of the—so-called Sorcerers."

Moltas reflected that the little tramp could be an *agent provocateur* sent by Asta to tempt him into heretical remarks. "So-called, Misur Brun?"

"We, uh, speak in confidence?"

"Certainly, if you wish it so."

"Old slave's gone to bed?"

"Probably. In any case he doesn't eavesdrop."

"Shit, they all do."

"He doesn't eavesdrop, Misur Brun."

"Sorry. Excuse it. Must be your nice wine. No offense, sir —thing is, I been in trouble once or twice before, from speaking out. Now what I mean, it's my opinion them ancient people weren't sorcerers at all, anyhow not like the northern witches. They was just people like us, only they had a lot of knowledge and skill that somehow got lost, that's all."

"I hope you're careful not to say such things openly."

"I ain't thirsting to look down on the fucking world from no cross, Deliberator."

"I have never put anyone in danger of the cross."

"I know that. 'Round the wharves they call you 'The Merciful.' "

"I earned that name," said Ian Moltas.

"Yes, sir—it's one way of looking at things. Me, I can see how the world's all fang and claw. Man's got to look out for himself, nobody else will." He took up his green sack. "Like to see something really good?" Moltas nodded, expecting trash.

The trader took out first a small tripod surmounted by a semicircular loop a foot high, the whole device one solid or welded piece of one of the ancient silver-gray metals impossible to reproduce in the modern age. He set this on the table, and then brought forth a flabby piece of what must be ancient Plassic in a curious flat harmony of mild colors, mostly blue and green and brown. At both ends of the lump were little metal devices. Brun placed one of these in his mouth, and puffed. Quickly the lump became a softly shining sphere. He placed it in the metal standard and tapped it so that it spun a long moment before quieting into rest. Moltas' mind whirled with it; as motion ceased he blinked and caught his breath.

"Gets you, don't it, sir? I picked it up in Penn from a collector who was afraid of owning it. That's why I could let you have it dirt cheap and still make a penny or two."

"But what is it?"

"A map."

"What are you saying?"

"The Sorcerers, if we got to call them that, knew that the world is round . . . The way it is up north, Deliberator, people believe that some of the Sorcerers, the Americans, are still around—you know, immortals, haunting devils. Church takes it seriously, or maybe"—his finger was laid again on his nose—"maybe it's just that keeping the devils in their place pays off. Useful things—like that kettle you got there—get the bad magic charmed out of 'em at so much a charm. I understand this was found in the cellar of some ruined building in the area near Fildelfia. The priests would've condemned it, but somebody grabbed it before they got there—"

"Round?"

"Ayah," said Brun with that unpleasant northern twang, and casually, as if dismissing something of no interest, but his eyes were too bright, too amused. "Pick it up if you like, Deliberator. It's not fragile—nor dangerous."

Ian Moltas did so, finding it astonishingly light. He touched the slick surface, so filled with soft splendor from the lamp, and the globe turned at his command. Without the twang, and without that undertone of sniggering laughter, Piet Brun said, "Your hands are holding up the world."

"You disturb me, sir. Naturally I am familiar with—certain philosophical theories."

"Sure." He was mocking again, or seemed to be. "Of course everyone knows the earth is flat."

Moltas was irritated. "On the contrary, there is obviously some curvature. One only need climb a hilltop—"

"Or go to sea, Deliberator, and watch the approach

of another ship: first the tip of her mast, and then the tops'l—"

"I know, I know. But after all—" He set the shining thing back on the table. "A map? Perhaps only the creation of an artist, a fanciful mind."

"Speaking of going to sea, Deliberator, what is the shipping situation in Norlenas at present?"

"Shipping? Why, I'm not too well-informed. Normal, I suppose."

"You see, I'm like a stranger here. I just might be interested in buying or chartering some kind of seagoing tub, but I don't know what kind of expense I'll be running into. If I ask around the docks, I won't get an honest answer, so I thought I'd ask you."

The flattery was harmless, and probably sincere. "I don't really know very much, Misur Brun. What sort of ship?"

"She ought to be a hundred-tonner, two-master, I think, with one-level galley and sound slaves—no Musons, I wouldn't give a shit for your Musons in an oar-bank—"

"Misur Brun, all galley rowers of Misipa are freemen. There are no slaves except the Musons."

"Do you tell me!"

"I'm surprised that as a Misipan born you should have forgotten."

"Well, I ran away at thirteen, and before then I didn't take note of much except to wonder when my old man would get drunk again and beat up on my ass. Well, not less than a hundred tons, and I don't want no coastwise crawler. Shorten her masts if I got to, and if her keel's no good I'll go for more ballast." Ian Moltas noticed for the first time that the fellow's clothes were rather good, even expensive, his fingernails clean, and his eyes, when not veiled in slyness, were those of a visionary, a listener to the winds. "Ride low and steady— you got to meet big water on its own terms."

"You think of trading with Velen in the south, perhaps?"

Piet Brun stared beyond him. "Perhaps."

"Well—not much more than guessing, sir—twelve thousand menin might buy you such a ship. About refitting and a cargo, I just don't know, couldn't advise you . . . And while we are on the subject of money, what would I have to pay for this—relic?"

Brun smiled at him. "Twelve thousand menin." The sphere was a poem of blue and green and brown, floating in the room's silence.

"If," said Moltas presently, "you plan to explore the possibility that the world is a sphere—which of course is not unfamiliar to the philosophers of the Tera, although regarded as far-fetched—won't you need this"—he touched the world and made it spin again—"this map?"

"Made me some tracings," Brun said. The smile was steady on his blunt face; whether the world was a sphere or the footstool of Sol-Amra, Piet Brun had a joke on it. "Made a copy on silk, that I can blow up to size with one of them pig's-bladder toys they make for the kids. Crude, but it'll serve my purpose."

"The thing is certainly a map, as you say. Some of these names I recognize as being old American—almost common knowledge that the City of God Norlenas was once called New Orleans. But your map shows it in the wrong place, and the line of the coast is absurd. The course of the Misipa ends —about here."

"Deliberator, the legends of the Flood are true legends. They know that, up in the north. At the southern end of the Hudson Sea there's a mighty heap of rubble, masses of tumbled masonry, here and there the top of a tower jutting from the water so heavily buttressed by trash and silt that the strongest seas and tides haven't leveled it. They call that place the Black Rocks, but everyone knows it's the ruins of the greatest city in what they call Old Time. The floods came, Deliberator, but they didn't drain away."

"I know the legends. Well, Misur Brun, your price for the relic is outrageous, almost comic, but I will even pay it. If that surprises you, set it down to the whim of an old man who cannot go exploring. I'll write you a draft on my—excuse me." Elkan had appeared in the archway from the hall, looking frightened. Moltas went to him.

"Sir, the Emperor has sent a litter with bearers."

"At this hour?"

Aware of the peddler, Elkan sank his voice to the barely audible. "A lieutenant of the Mavid is with them."

"An escort, no doubt," said Ian Moltas, who knew better. Lieutenants of Asta's secret police were not sent on small errands of courtesy. "I'll go down presently. Has Madam Moltas come back from that banquet?"

"Not yet, sir."

"Bring me my jewel case from the strongbox in my bedroom, Elkan." He returned to his visitor. "Misur Brun, it will be best if I pay you with a jewel of about that value. You've come back to Misipa at a very unstable time. Men go out of favor swiftly, sometimes die swiftly—curious times, very curious. It's possible—so quickly do fortunes change—you might have difficulty cashing a draft tomorrow morning, even though I have plenty of funds to cover it. But jewels will remain negotiable."

"Sir, whatever is convenient." Brun was flushed, still thrown off balance by the incredible success of his errand; it occurred to Moltas that he might have asked that price simply as a piece of impudence, a joke, a conversation piece to introduce genuine bargaining.

"Thank you, Elkan. Here—if you will take this to any appraiser in White Cradle Street, Misur Brun—"

"Sir, I would never question the Deliberator's—"

"I have a litter waiting for me, a late errand. Perhaps I could take you part way to wherever you're staying? Go ahead, please—I'll follow in a moment."

He needed that moment with Elkan, to stand there eye to eye, and hold out his hand as one does to any friend and equal. "I'll return, I suppose," he said. Elkan hesitated long; then the grasp of the six-fingered hand was firm and to Moltas very strange, a bridge between worlds that must somehow communicate with friendship, or die.

The lieutenant of the Mavid politely and correctly pointed out that the litter was small, with no room for anyone but himself and his passenger. A genteel, patient man, in his black loincloth and black tunic with the emblem of crossed spears. Piet Brun spoke a mannerly goodbye, and walked jauntily down the dark street with a green emerald fortune in his pocket that might have bought the virtue of even a Mavid lieutenant. "We are going to the palace, I presume, Lieutenant?"

"Yes, sir. Why are you laughing, my lord, may I ask?"

"I could never explain it," said Ian Moltas.

The scrawny little body of Asta, Appointed of Sol-Amra, Lord of the World, defied the silken ease of his chair, incapable of relaxation; his tight face betrayed a hunger no world could satisfy. The audience room was cool and lovely under the mild lamps, the floor a mosaic of priceless imported marble, gray and rose. A naked Muson girl with a fixed smile held a platter of fruit near his chair, and Asta chewed raisins as if they were the flesh of enemies. "Sit if you wish, Deliberator."

A hundred and fifty years ago, when Ocasta, first of the Emperors, was crowned, the privileges of the Deliberators had been written into statute: an attempt of those who loved the Republic to retain some color of it when the reality was gone. Moltas could have taken the low stool, the only other seat in the room, without need of permission. That Asta had granted it was one of those petty victories the Emperor needed as some need coffee or marawan. And to remain standing would have been bad politics. "Manners, child!" said Asta, and gave the girl a brutal push toward Moltas, who took a fig and nibbled it for politics' sake.

She was small and pretty, like a child indeed at first glance, but Moltas could not guess her age. The platter was heavy, her thin arms in danger of trembling. Asta was known to enjoy the sterile delights of maintaining a harem of Muson women, his Empress being no more to him than a breeder of sons for the dynasty; and rumor had it that any of the girls who survived a few months of his pleasures were given to specially favored members of the ruling clique, as marks of the Emperor's esteem—disposable, in fact, like towels.

"Moltas"—the Emperor sighed with staged patience— what do you *want*, man? A year ago, we recollect, we offered you a Treasury post—no sinecure, responsible work you could have done very well."

"Majesty, I felt that an elective post was a trust I could not abandon. My talent is in the framing and interpretation of law."

"We know that's what you say. Law and policy, hey?"

A tricky question. In theory, the Assembly might still debate imperial policy; in practice, the Emperor disregarded it. The Emperor proposed measures; if the Assembly did not ratify them they still became law, humorously described as Statutes of Misipa A.D.—Assembly Dissenting. But should the Assembly adopt measures unwelcome to the Emperor, his veto was final. The Assembly was a ghost, a graveyard of honor. One power remained to it, an intangible—the strangely passionate, inarticulate veneration the people still held for it as a symbol of an older time. Even in these sour years memory would not quite die, and A.D. laws were resented—blindly and ineffectively, yet the resentment was real, and the ruler of an explosive people could not wholly disregard it. Moltas said with an evasiveness Asta would understand, "Majesty, the Assembly's position on policy seems to require a day-to-day definition."

Asta smiled clammily and let that pass. "Well—not long ago, we offered you a title. Because we wished to make use of your unquestioned talents on the Advisory Council. You declined. We have been very patient with you, Moltas."

"I felt, Majesty, that a transfer to the Advisory Council would place me out of touch with the people, the citizens—"

Asta leaned forward, waggling a schoolteacher's forefinger. "Are you proposing to instruct us concerning the *people*, Ian Moltas? Don't you understand even yet that the people have one true friend, one only—the Emperor? Why do you think we are known as the Humanitarian, the Light-Bringer of Sol-Amra?"

Moltas thought: *off and running. This could take half an hour.*

It was less than that, but the sentences rolled on like chariot wheels, and a vision appeared of the world as Asta saw it: the Misipan Empire expanding to the utmost, old Velen beyond the Southern Sea crushed, occupied, absorbed as far as the jungles at the lower rim of the world; the northern lands punished for their arrogance by Misipan crossbow and phalanx, Katskil industry harnessed to the Misipan chariot, Misipan law and custom and religion extending at last to all the limits of the earth—one state, one shining whole, dissent unknown and the Humanitarian sitting on top of it. "The state, Moltas—what is there but the state? Do you talk to us of the people, when our vision alone can see them as they are? Ants in a colony, leaves of a tree that perish to enrich the earth." Asta broke off, tightly smiling. "We forget you live on a diet of oratory. To business. We have a special project in mind, Moltas, and we are convinced that there are few other—ants—in the Empire who could do it as well as yourself. We are correct in thinking that you are much concerned with the welfare of the Musons? Even to the point of desiring certain changes in the ancient laws? This is true, sir?"

"It is true, Majesty. I think everyone knows it. Of course, the present temper of the times—"

"My dear Moltas, damn the times. Great men—and deities —make the times. I am the times, Ian Moltas. Now, we have in mind a definitive study of the entire institution of Muson slavery—a work of true scholarship . . . done under our auspices, of course, but without any interference with your scholarly efforts—to serve as a basis for intelligent recommendations leading to improvement. We are quite aware of —let us say, inequities, even cruelties, I'm sorry to say; and you ought to understand that the welfare of the Musons has always been close to our heart. Now we propose that you undertake this study—no restrictions of course, all facilities, any type of assistance you wish, in addition to our promise to give the closest consideration to any recommendations you make." *The tiger invites me to his den for this tainted tidbit —why? What does he want, that requires bringing me here after midnight, when he himself is red-eyed from lack of sleep?* "We have looked into the difficulties, Moltas, and find no legal objection to your assuming this task while retaining your status as Deliberator, with leave of absence."

"Majesty, are there other conditions?"

Asta caught the little slave's buttock and jerked her body to emphasize his words. "See, darling, see how they mistrust me, these everlasting politicians! Notice it, darling? Never fails." She achieved a dutiful giggle, trying to keep her tray of fruit from spilling. A ripe plum rolled and splatted on the floor by Asta's foot. "Clumsy idiot bitch!" The Appointed of Sol-Amra sent the girl staggering to the floor with a blow on the breast; a wave of his arm fetched a guard from the anteroom to pick her up and carry her out of sight. "Some of 'em aren't worth training," Asta said, "but she may do well enough at the farm. Seems healthy. I forget, Moltas," said the Emperor, who never forgot anything, "do you keep a Muson stud?"

Ian Moltas counted to eight. His marriage had not been blessed with children; he thanked God for it. "No, Majesty, that is a project I have never attempted."

"You might find it illuminating for the study we hope you'll undertake. Pity they're so long-lived and come so late to fertility—makes it difficult to experiment with bloodlines. Well, well, you mentioned conditions. Yes, honored Deliberator, we are attaching one condition, and if you suppose the gods themselves could rule men without a little horse-trading, honored Deliberator, your lifetime in politics has been spent in vain. Tomorrow a measure of considerable importance will be presented to the Assembly. It will not be well received, but it happens to be vital to larger considerations of Empire, and an A.D. law, honored Deliberator, will not do! Now, we have noted that some seventeen of the thirty-nine Deliberators have consistently opposed our best efforts toward the welfare of Misipa—obstructionists, reactionaries, selfish old men without vision. Perhaps a dozen others genuinely understand the necessities of the empire that must soon govern the world. The rest—waverers, sheep, *pliable* old men, whom you could sway in the direction of enlightenment. Tomorrow we wish to have your vote on the right side."

"The Emperor would allow a definitive study of Muson slavery to depend on a single political action of one Deliberator?" And Moltas wondered whether the guards would be in for him. He had spoken his unforgivable words in a mild voice; it was even possible that Asta was too stupid to understand all the implications.

Asta had not failed to understand. As he bent forward a flush of blood grew up around his eyes and receded; his voice also was soft. "You may have missed the point, Deliberator Moltas. We ought to have said: we *prefer* to have your vote on the right side—but don't exaggerate your importance . . . What is your final answer?"

"Majesty, if I may, I should like to consider my answer overnight. Then my vote in the Assembly can be taken as my answer."

"I see. Very well." Asta relaxed, sighing with histrionic patience. "Perhaps you should remember that your vote is not in any way necessary—no more necessary, after all, than the Assembly itself or the continued health of its members. You may go."

Elkan was waiting to open the door, a ritual service he valued. "Elkan, when you spoke with Misur Brun before you brought him up to me, did he mention where he was staying?"

"Yes, sir. The Sign of the Fox, on Dasin Street. It's cheap but respectable."

"Curious fellow. And what a curious thing is a scale of values! The palace is in a poisonous mood, Elkan, and the Assembly may not survive tomorrow."

Elkan stood with folded hands; but when Moltas said no more, he took a torch from a bracket and went ahead to light the Deliberator's way up the marble stairs. "Sir, I ventured to set up another table in the museum."

"Ah, thank you!" Passing through the archway into the museum he saw Elkan's work at once, for the sphere of the world stood on the new table, and before it was the two-faced image. At each end of the table burned a lamp, and all other lamps were extinguished; thus the slave had said: *Here is the world, and here is man, and here is an imperfect light.* "Thank you and good night, Elkan."

He sat before the world in the half-dark, and though the idea of a round earth was perverse, grotesque, even ridiculous, somewhere there might be a truth in it. The sun moves in the heavens, does it not? The sun and the moon? Suppose those orbs are vastly greater than they appear to us. Then imagine some being existing on the surface of one of them:

would not our sphere—our *sphere*—seem to his eyes as
does the sun or the moon to ours? But if all things are in
motion—

*It is too much. If all things move and flow—if nothing is
ever stable, but all creation is journeying—*

Someone entered the museum with a rustling of a skirt—
Keva, who would be distressed at his wakefulness. "Ian,
aren't you coming to bed? (The banquet was a deadly bore,
deadly.) How can you go on without sleep?" He leaned his
head back against her breast. "Oh, I suppose it's politics,
politics. I wish you wouldn't take so many cares on yourself.
No rest?"

"Trouble brewing for the Assembly itself. It may blow
over."

"Don't let things distress you so much."

"It's my life, Keva."

"You went to the palace, Elkan told me."

"Asta wishes me to make a scholarly study of Muson slavery."

"Why, that's wonderful!—isn't it? You'd be relieved from
the Assembly? And it's something you want to do, isn't it?"

"A condition is attached. And the study itself would end in
nothing but one more recommendation."

"I see. I suppose I see."

"What do you see, my dear?"

"I see that in order to satisfy some—some impossible standard of virtue, you're about to throw the Emperor's offer back
in his face, never mind if it means your neck, your neck— I
can't understand you. I never did understand you. This room,
all those old things, dead things—oh, I see you brood and
don't know where your mind is. Ian, we must live in the
present, isn't it so?"

"It's a flash between infinities, a place to be happy and sad.
It's not true that the present is the only place we know. I
must look beyond, both ways. I can't change myself—"

"Ah, no more, let's not talk about it. Don't stay up much longer, Ian—please? My God, it'll be dawn in an hour or two."

"I'll come to bed soon, Keva."

"What's that absurd round thing?"

"A toy perhaps. Age of the Sorcerers. Go and rest, Keva."

When he was alone again Moltas remembered how some of the stars move, or seem to, like the sun and moon. One lamp was still burning at the palace, a busy, baleful eye; beyond it, the serenity of the dark.

The morning came heavy with wet heat and a hint of storm. In the lobby of the Assembly Hall lounged five of the Mavid with sword and dagger and riot club, neat in their black loincloths and tunics, pointedly disregarding the arriving Deliberators. By every tradition they had no right there; by an even older and graver custom, weapons were forbidden in the Assembly Hall. Moltas felt on his arm the touch of a friend, Amid Anhur; liver spots showed on the crinkled hand—Amid was old, too old, like many here. An evil of the day, no fault of Asta's, that only the rich could afford to try for election in this land that still believed itself to have a representative government, under an emperor who meant to restore the Republic any day; and few of the young were rich. Amid said, "I suppose we must ignore the vermin, Ian? Merely a squad of the wolf's personal fleas."

"How long can we hold out?"

"A day—a week—a year."

"How many of us still possess our souls?"

The building was the work of the middle Republic; Amid Anhur stared at a groove in the threshold of the inner doorway, worn there by more than two hundred years of passage of Misipa's lawmakers. "A year ago I think I could have said twenty-four. Now, Barshon and Menefar dead—possibly of natural causes. The younger Samis murdered in a tavern, the

Mavid not curious about his murderers, while his father remembers he has one more son. See Carmon there, pretending not to know I nodded to him. You and I are not safe to know."

"Come to my house this evening. I've bought a curious thing."

"Another antiquity? What about today, Ian?"

"This thing is timeless. I beg you come, have dinner with us. Keva would be happy to see you."

"Oh, I will come, gladly," said the old man, and they entered the hall. "We should concern ourselves with timeless things—while we have a little time."

Kalon Samis, month's Moderator, called them to order, his voice flat and schooled and careful, perhaps in memory of a son. There should have been continuation of a debate on the silk tax, but a sheet of parchment was quivering in Samis' fingers. "There is an imperial message which I am directed to read before the day's business." At the back of the hall a Mavid captain leaned against the bronze doors, his presence unprotested by anything more than angry glances and shocked disdain. "And gentlemen, my reading of this message is to be taken as a motion: formal debate may follow, but perhaps it should be limited. The message reads: 'It is the Imperial intention that the Assembly recognize second and third cousins and cousins by marriage of the Emperor as full members of the Imperial household, entitled to serve not only on the Advisory Council by reason of nobility, but also as consultant members of the Assembly of Deliberators, each to have one vote.' Now as I have said, debate should be limited."

Moltas was on his feet. Some others would soon have broken the stunned and nauseated silence—already he could hear choked words and heavy breathing—but Samis recognized him with a feeble nod. "Deliberators of Misipa, there are occasions when men may find it best not to accept a kick in the groin with murmurs of polite thanks. It is my view—"

It was not difficult, so long as he was on his feet and following the momentum of his own expert and powerful voice. The Assembly had always enjoyed rounded periods and poetic thunder, a part of the style—antique perhaps, but there was a place for it. And now, if a man chose to risk binding himself to the cross in the marketplace with a rope of words, the Assembly would hear him out courteously while he did it. "The cousins, it is true, may find our little gathering a bore at times—dull debates, tax laws, arguments, so many things to interfere with scratching or lifting the tail of a close friend." He introduced other jests and obscenities, although his ears told him that what little laughter responded was merely that of nervousness close to hysteria. Still, in a way they liked it—hanged men dance.

There was relaxation through the mass of well-known faces when he began to speak of the Republic. It was an Assembly cliché, to look toward that lost time with a nostalgia rendered harmless by futility. But then they understood that Moltas was not speaking in that manner. He was speaking of the Republic as if it were a living place almost within the here and now—over a hill; a day's journey. He was asking them to think that what citizens have built once and lost, they may build again, a little better with good fortune. There were times, he said, when human effort appeared to generate nothing but suffering, error, confusion—but maybe even these times add a little to the sum of human understanding. "And there are times," said Ian Moltas, "when the will to struggle against evil seems to be altogether gone. This may be such a time. If the Assembly perishes, there will be no light until, somewhere in the land, you see light from the fires of revolution—not you, perhaps, for most of you will not be there. And now I say, only to a few of you: we need not be ashamed if sometimes there is nothing better to do for an idea than to die for it."

The Assembly voted against Asta, twenty to eighteen. Samis abstained.

The Mavid captain was a trained speaker too. He strode front, ignoring Moderator Samis, and waited for his correct instant of silence. "By decree of Asta, Appointed of Sol-Amra, Lord of the World, the Assembly of Deliberators now stands dissolved. You will not leave the boundaries of holy Norlenas, and will consider yourselves under the Emperor's displeasure until he has examined certain charges brought against individual members of this body. You will leave the building quietly and go to your homes. That is all."

No longer sustained by the courage of action, his thoughts fluttered like startled doves. *Keva—what can I do?—she has relatives in the Imperial family—maybe—*

Elkan—there is the will—but he will go—money for Elkan —if only—

Sign of the Fox in Dasin Street. Why, I will go and arrange with that fellow—might we not sail—you've got to meet big water on its own terms—

But the Mavid captain had a particular message for him, halting him on the steps of the hall, with two of his men, in case there should be difficulties. Moltas said, "Gentlemen, the world is a sphere."

The captain said neutrally, "You are to come for questioning to the prison in the Seventh Ward."

One of the men was very young, almost a boy. "I will come without resistance, of course," Moltas said, but he wanted to address the boy. "You see, if the world is a sphere, life becomes interesting again—does it not? So much more to know. Do you understand?" The young face showed only alarm.

"We want no difficulty," said the captain, and locked Moltas' wrists behind him.

"Don't you understand, boy? If the world is a sphere, it may also be a star."

THE LEGEND OF
COUGAR LOU LANDIS

by Edward Bryant

     Each of Edward Bryant's stories of the gleaming city named Cinnabar is complete and delightful in itself, but as the story shards multiply they blend together into a fascinating mosaic of our far future; ultimately Bryant plans to collect them as a book. Meanwhile, we've had "Jade Blue" in Universe 1, *and now "The Legend of Cougar Lou Landis," a deceptively rich story about the wellsprings of heroism. Cinnabar is a near-magical city; you wouldn't think of anyone as poor if she had the money to buy its technological wonders. But some people will always need more.*

THE GARDENER Yakov lay dying in the desert gravel. He sprawled on his left side, eyes to the east, where he watched the stars blur above Cinnabar. Oh, for warmth. Was this how it was to die of cold? Yakov had always believed freezing to be a slow decline into gentle sleep. There was first the sharp bite of frost, yes. But then came the sleepy arrival of death. Not for Yakov; he had lain alert for hours. The gravel chaffed his skin unbearably. The beating administered him by his master had broken bones. Yakov moaned softly and prayed the cold to kill.

There was an answer on the wind. Yakov listened intently. Was it his master, returning to inflict more pain? Yakov tried to pull gravel over himself, to darken the shadows in which he hid. The wind brought the voice again, closer this time. "Is someone there? Who is it?"

Yakov pulled at the small rocks with his one good hand. He whimpered in spite of himself.

"I hear you. You're at the foot of the dune. What's the matter?"

A figure rose up in the night and bent over him. Frightened, Yakov flinched and closed his eyes. Hair softly tickled across his face.

"You're hurt, aren't you?" Fingers gently touched the gardener's shattered limbs.

Yakov opened his eyes and blinked, trying to focus. "Who are you?"

"I'm a friend." The voice was low and sympathetic. The woman's fingers continued to probe carefully. "Lie perfectly still."

"It hurts very much," said Yakov.

"*. . . hurts very much.*"

"*Is it worth the pain?*" *asked her mother.*

She stared at her hands, flexing the fingers repeatedly,

then made a fist. She extended the index finger and brought it slowly toward her nose. The finger touched her upper lip and she recoiled. "It's worth the pain," she affirmed. "The strangeness is something else again."

"I think you're dying."

"I know. I've wanted to die for hours."

"You're cold," said the woman. She pulled a piece of clothing, soft and warm, over Yakov. She flicked a lighter. "I'm afraid there's no kindling for a fire out here."

Yakov stared at her face. "I know you. I've heard of you. You're Cougar Lou." With a tired wonder he looked at her long, tawny hair and wide, violet eyes. Then the flame went out. "Will you help me?"

"You know that you're dying."

"I want vengeance."

"Who did this?"

"Josephus the Administrator. I worked in his greenhouse. His favorite orchids were the flaming moths. Somehow they died of rust. Josephus was furious."

"The son of a bitch," said Cougar Lou.

"I think it's getting colder."

"I wish I had more than my cape. I'm sorry."

"I'm glad I met you." Yakov choked on the blood and twisted his head aside to spit.

"Would you like that bastard to die?"

The operating theater glittered like sunlight on snow. She felt like dying; then remembered how soon, how grandly she would live.

Yakov made a twisted smile in the darkness.

"Now lie back," said Cougar Lou. "I can make it easier for you."

Yakov coughed rackingly. He brought his knees up in the fetal position. "Too late. . . ."

"No," she said. "Here." Cougar Lou pressed a metal cube tightly against the gardener's temple. His body spasmed.

Yakov the gardener:
 akov the gardener:B
  kov the gardener:Br
   ov the gardener:Bro
    v the gardener:Bros
     the gardener:Brosk
     the gardener:Broskl
     he gardener:Broskla
      e gardener:Brosklaw
       gardener:Brosklaw
        ardener:Brosklaw t
         dener:Brosklaw th
          ener:Brosklaw the
           ner:Brosklaw the c
            er:Brosklaw the ch
             r:Brosklaw the chi
              :Brosklaw the chie
               Brosklaw the chief

It broke open, pushed free, gulped alien air, and wished somatically for the soothing liquid to return. Wailing, the baby was slapped, bathed, wrapped, and rocked. Later, it fed.

"Do!" he said, pointing. A proud voice: "He said it—his first word."

Another time, the second word: "Get!"

The pride of parents: so precious, so bright. "We love you." And they rocked him every time he cried.

"Brosie, Brosie," said playmate Kenneth. "Little baby Brosie." Kenneth was twice Brosklaw's size; Brosklaw hit him with a rock.

"Brosklaw, you will go far," said his mother.

"Listen to your mother," said his father.

They pushed him, stimulated him with books and tapes and holos. Not too much music, though. Very little art. He became extremely capable and knowledgeable, and even suspected how good he really was.

"Brosklaw, you will go far," said his tutor. "Just continue to apply yourself."

By adolescence, he retained a long string of lovers.

"Sometimes I wonder what I'm doing here with you," mused Tourmaline Hayes, the sex star. "Morbid curiosity?"

He laughed and made love to her again.

"Only the best education," said his father. "Selden University."

"The police?" said his mother.

"Real power is the control of human behavior," quoted her son.

"You've got everything you want," said each of his wives at one time or another. "What more?"

"I have everything I wanted," he corrected them. "As I grow older I discover new things to desire."

"Chief of police of Craterside Park," his mother said, during a visit. "That's impressive for one so young."

Brosklaw smiled.

His mother said, "When will you move up to city administration?"

"That's coming."

Brosklaw walked down one of the clean, well-lighted streets of Craterside Park. A woman stepped from between two spiral towers and confronted him. He stared at the lithe body. "Don't I know you?" he said. "You're—"

Yakov the gardener shook convulsively a final time and died. Cougar Lou took the cold piece of metal away from his head. She retrieved her cape and watched him for a while. In the starlight, Yakov was barely visible against the gravel.

". . . rather be anybody than who I am." She looked defiantly at her mother.

"Your adolescence has been prolonged," said Anita.

She picked up a film-viewer and hurled it at the wall. The viewer exploded in a thousand shining pieces.

"Don't do that," said Anita mildly. She put her hand to the cut on her forehead, and one finger came away red.

Cougar Lou shivered and rubbed her hands together. They were sticky with Yakov's blood. It was real, and the smell of it made her sick.

The quiet of a Craterside Park night was shattered by the sound of a man attacking a sculpture in one of the district's many scenic parks. The statue was the heroic stylization of a mastodon. Its massive feet were anchored solidly in a base. It could not move, other than to wind its trunk back and squirt water at its attacker. The man leaned against the statue's haunch, repeatedly driving a fist into its ribs. The sound boomed hollowly. The sculpture honked in distress and discharged another ineffective stream.

Eventually, Craterside Park residents anonymously contacted the police. A patrol car whispered up to the square and set down. The two cops approached the mastodon's assailant warily.

"Hey!" said the short cop. "Stop that. Turn around and keep your hands in plain sight."

The second patrolman hefted his stunner, just in case.

The man slowly turned at the cop's voice. He stared at the patrolmen vaguely. Hulking, he was at least a head taller than either cop.

"Easy," warned the first cop. "Take it slow."

They shined their lights in the man's face.

The first cop gasped. "Chief Brosklaw? Is that you?"

"Chief?" said the second cop. He took a step closer.

"Chief?" echoed the man. "Chief?" His jaw hung slack. He turned back to the stylized mastodon and again began to pound its flank, the boom resounding far across Craterside Park.

Mary Elouise Olvera-Landis returned home quite early in the morning. She let herself into the huge old house on Feldspar Drive quietly. Only one of her contract husbands greeted her. "Are Nels and Richard asleep?" she asked.

Macy got up from the couch in front of the fireplace and stretched. "They didn't last past midnight."

Lou kissed him. She tried to play no favorites, but Macy held an edge in her affections. He was the practical one of her husbands, thinking rather than feeling. She often sensed he was troubled, as though trying to find his way out of imaginary labyrinths. Richard, her second husband, was undisciplined and lustful. She found him exciting. The third, Nels, was ethereally worshipful, but usually preoccupied with his researches at the Tancarae Institute.

"Where have you been?"

"Out," she said.

"Cards at your family's?"

She put her hands to her throat and unbuckled the cape. "I took the windhover out to the greenbelt. I wanted to walk alone in the desert."

Smiling, he said, "Did you find a burning bush?" Macy was a librarian and knew all the old stories.

She shook her head. "I found a dying man."

"Anyone we know?"

"Don't joke," she snapped. "He was a stranger."

"I thought it might be your flair for drama."

She nodded. "You're right; it was a fiction. Forget it."

"Do you want a drink?"

"Something hot. No stimulants."

They sat by the fireplace and drank mint tea. "How long until morning?" Lou asked.

"Three hours, maybe four."

"I want to sleep here by the fireplace."

"Carpet's filthy. Nels didn't clean yesterday."

"He forgot," Lou said.

"Well, it's still dirty."

"I'll put my cape down," she mocked. "Do you mind?"

"I'm not finicky." He reached for her. She allowed him to draw her down. After they had made love, the artificial logs still burned brightly. "Turn down the fire," said Macy sleepily.

Lou twisted the valve. "Are you tired?"

"Yes." He nuzzled against her like a child, left leg thrown over her waist.

"I'm not sleepy."

He opened one eye. "What do you want?"

She smiled ingenuously. "A story."

Macy groaned and sat up. "Once upon a time, there was a brave woman named Robin Hood . . ."

In the dim light of the fireplace, Macy looked exasperated. "Aren't you tired yet?"

She shook her head.

"You're worse than any child. All right, what do you want to talk about?"

"Anything."

He considered. "Since I'm the newest of your husbands, let's talk about you."

"All right."

"There's a hologram in your room. Is that your sister?"

She was quiet for a few moments. "I didn't expect that."

"You don't have to answer."

"The hologram is not my sister. It's me."

His voice was surprised. "She looks nothing like you."

"For convenience," the surgeon said, "we have standard patterns."

She shook her head. "I brought my own specifications."

"The family's prosperous," said Lou. "We can purchase wonders. Have you any idea what I was like as a child?"

"You were extroverted, bright, and athletic. I imagine you were the center of all interest here in Craterside Park."

"Wrong. I was bright, but I was also clumsy and fat. I was introverted to the point of catatonia. Months and months I wouldn't go out of the house. I spent my time reading and viewing heroic fantasies—Joan of Arc, Robin Hood, Gerry Cornelius, all of them. I imagined I was all sorts of other people living in different times."

"Escapist."

"Didn't you ever dream?"

"Of course."

"Of what?"

He considered the question. "I don't remember."

"I dreamed I was a hero. I saw myself as strong and lithe as a cougar. One birthday, my parents gave me all that. It took months for the restructuring. Months more for physical training."

Macy looked intrigued. "That holo—The difference is incredible."

"Sometimes I wish I were her again."

"That's stupid." He gently kissed a line along her jaw. "You're beautiful now."

"Would you feel that if I were still her?"

He hesitated. "I think so."

"You only approach honesty." She laughed. "You're so damned politic."

"Beautiful Cougar Lou."

"What?"

"You dreamed of being a cougar. Cougar Lou. It fits."

"It does," Lou murmured, almost as a question. "It's almost morning. Let's make love again."

Before sunrise, they moved to the tall windows facing east.

Better than lying with a book in an invented world?

He raised his head. "Did you say something?"

She shook her head slowly. "Do you know," said Macy, "that you talk in your sleep?"

The elder matriarch of the Olvera-Landis family arrived shortly after noon. Lou greeted her mother at the door. "Good afternoon, Mary Elouise," said Anita. "Are your husbands about?"

"Macy is out," Lou said. "Nels is at the institute and Richard is with a party hunting for sea snark."

"Fine. I wish to talk with you alone." She led Lou to the parlor. "This is nothing you haven't heard before."

"I expected that."

"The family has been talking," said Anita. "We are worried about you. Don't you think that perhaps this house is a little large for you to manage?"

"I have three husbands."

"And aren't they also perhaps a bit too much?"

"I can manage."

"Can you really, dear?" She placed a plump hand on her daughter's wrist. "You are young and willful, Mary Elouise, but that will carry you only so far. What are you going to *do?*"

"I'll live here." Lou stared at the carpet, following patterns. "I intend to help people."

"Heroes?" Macy once laughed. "Heroines? Killers and thieves—outlaws."

In a rage, she ordered him from her bed.

Anita laughed. "My dear, machines are for helping people. People have better things to do."

Lou kept a stubborn silence.

"The family is reluctant to continue supporting you in this fashion. You've had a nice fling. Now come home."

"Into the family business?"

"If you'd like. We won't force you."

"And my husbands?"

"Three seems a bit extravagant. Can't you keep—" She rolled her shoulders. "Oh, just one?"

"So will you marry me?"

"The terms are good," said Macy. *"Why not?"*

"Is that all?"

"This isn't Le Morte d'Arthur, *love."*

"Mother, may I think about it?"

"Again? I suppose so. But you'll have to return soon. The expense, you know. Supporting a separate house in Crater-side Park is so ridiculous. You can't expect these birthday extravagances to last forever."

"I realize that."

"Then I'll talk to you again soon." Anita rose to leave. "Oh, did you hear about our fine police chief?"

"What about him?"

"I saw it on Network this morning. He was picked up by his own men last night. He attempted to damage a nocturnal sculpture in one of the squares."

"How odd," said Lou.

"Indeed. Even stranger, it seems his entire memory is gone. The police suspect foul play."

"Craterside Park used to be so peaceful."

Her mother agreed. "These days, I don't know what we're coming to."

After Anita left, Lou went to her special room. No one slept with her there. It was a retreat. The floor undulated over circulating liquid. The walls opened into infinitely expanded holovistas. Today Lou chose trees. She was surrounded by brooding, illusory forests. She lay down on the forest floor.

How blessed to rest. She still dreamed as Cougar Lou, but when she woke, could not remember those dreams.

She dozed, but did not sleep, and came awake disoriented and confused. She stared at the underbrush, wishing that once, just once, an unprogrammed animal would come slinking out to greet her. Lou turned over and watched clouds traverse the high-resolution blue sky.

Steal from the rich, give to the poor . . . That had come from Macy and the dusty, tattered pages of an ancient book.

What am I doing? she thought. How can I re-create a past that probably never existed? Whom am I helping helping helping helping . . .

Wake up, wake up, whispered the night wind. Lou jerked upright. "All right," she said. "I'm awake." The forests blinked out and Lou was alone in the small gray room.

Outside, Nels waited for her. He was clearly agitated. "I'm sorry," he said. "I thought you ought to know. Macy and Richard are fighting."

She rubbed her eyes. "What about?"

"You."

"I'm still asleep," Lou said. "Why should they fight over me?"

"Come on," said Nels. He tugged her toward the hallway.

"Why me?"

Nels stumbled over the words. "It's your family. We heard you're going back. You'll keep only one husband—"

"Let's go." They hurried along the corridor, Nels's bony legs pacing her. "Who told you?"

Nels looked at her uncomfortably. "It was my cousin Ingrid. Her maid's aunt is second housekeeper to the Olvera-Landis household. The aunt heard a discussion about you at dinner and couldn't keep it to herself." He ducked his head. "I'm sorry. I told Richard; then he and Macy got into it."

"They're idiots," Lou said.

They clattered down the main stairs. Richard and Macy were in the dining hall. The table had been shoved to one side and the two men stood in the cleared space. Each was clad only in a pair of baggy white pantaloons, tied securely at waist and ankles. The two men jumped up and down, screaming epithets.

Lou stopped at the bottom of the flight. She wondered whether to laugh. "What are they doing?"

"Their pantaloons," Nels said, pointing. "Each of them dropped a resurrectronic ferret in there. The first one whose ferret gnaws its way free through the cloth wins."

"That's stupid!" Lou cried. She ran into the dining hall and grabbed Macy's shoulder. Without taking his eyes from Richard's face, he shoved her aside.

"Leave us be," said Richard. He was stocky, with long arms and head as smooth as a desert stone.

High-pitched squeaks came from the men's trousers.

"Idiots!" Lou screamed. "When the ferrets are through, neither one of you'll be fit for a husband!"

"Get away," said Macy. "We have to settle it. First us; then Nels."

"Nels, help me stop them." Lou grabbed one of the spindly dining-room chairs and smashed it at a suspicious bulge on Macy's calf. Her husband yelled and fell sideways. Something jerked and twitched under the fabric of his pantaloons. Lou swung again with the broken chair leg and heard sophisticated circuitry break.

"Damn you," said Macy. He reached to stop her hand. She kicked him in the face.

Lou turned and found Nels and Richard rolling on the floor. Nels's legs were locked around Richard's waist. Jackknifed forward, he pummeled a lump on Richard's ankle.

"Richard! It's over." Her second husband glared up at her, then took his hands away from Nels' throat.

The four people surveyed one another. Macy wiped his bloody nose with his hand. Lou gave him a napkin from the sideboard. Nels massaged his own throat gingerly. Richard sat up, looking sullen.

"You stupid pricks," said Lou. "Is Nels the only one with any sense?"

"It's true, then? You're going back to your family?" Richard demanded.

"Who gets discarded?" said Macy.

"Anita came to see me today. That's what she wanted."

"So what are you going to do?"

"I haven't decided. But I do know I don't want you fighting over me like stud bulls."

"Aren't you the great romantic?" Macy said spitefully.

Lou turned on him. "No, not this way. Now all of you, get out. Just leave me alone."

The three men stared at her. "Do you want to see any of us later on tonight?" Richard asked.

She shook her head. "I'm sore and I want to be alone." Lou turned back toward the stairs. They watched until she disappeared past the upper landing.

She sat on the topmost parapet of the highest turret of the old house and dangled her feet into space. She drew the cloak about herself. The simulated cougar fur was proof against the night wind off the ocean.

Who am I? she thought. I'm Cougar Lou Landis.

No, replied Mary Elouise Olvera-Landis. I'm an ugly, awkward girl who finds only vicarious marvels. My heroes are in books and tapes and story computers. I am locked inside a walking fantasy. But that doesn't change me. I'm still Mary Elouise.

I'm the new reality, thought Cougar Lou. I exist in my strength and grace.

You will always be Mary Elouise, answered Mary Elouise. No. No?

Cougar Lou stared out toward City Center where the stars twinkled faster and became a blur. Tomorrow, she thought, Anita will return for me. I'm such a child; I'll do as she asks.

I wish I were the hero I've pretended.

The scattered lights of Craterside Park spread below her. One of the tiny stars marked the home of Josephus the Administrator. "Yakov," she whispered. "Little gardener, you're my last chance for self-respect."

Cougar Lou stood and balanced easily on the stone parapet. . . . *steps. Stairs were the hardest. At first, the new perspectives came slowly. She stepped or reached, and often missed. The fine, lithe body throbbed with new bruises.* She looped one end of a line around a crenelation and knotted it. Then she tossed the coil into the darkness. She clipped the rope around the break-bar secured to her belt, then looped the rope around her hips and began to rappel silently down from the tower.

As a young girl, she had attended garden parties at Josephus' estate. Cougar Lou knew the route. She took alleyways and climbed over rooftops, avoiding Craterside Park's safe streets.

Two patrolmen sat telling each other ghost stories beside the gateway to Josephus' estate. ". . . out of the closet, jaws gaping . . ." The words floated across as she crawled through the shrubbery.

Cougar Lou anticipated little difficulty in getting to Josephus. There would be few safeguards. Craterside Park was relatively free of wrongdoing. The patrolmen patrolled because Chief Brosklaw had liked good appearances.

Once past the gateway, she ran across the checkerboard lawns. She reached the back of the house. A window turned silently inward and Cougar Lou let herself into Josephus' kitchen. Pausing to orient herself to the new darkness, she searched back through her adolescence and remembered the master bedroom was on the second floor, south wing. Negotiating the stairs and hallways took a few minutes. Soon she was in front of the correct door. She slid it aside and took a cold metal cube from her belt-pouch.

"*. . . brought us memories of a better life. Why?*"

She looked away from twisted limbs and shriveled souls. "You've never had riches."

They stared at her.

Lights glared on. Across the room, Josephus sat up in bed

and smiled at her. "Mary Elouise, how nice to see you. You were expected."

Cougar Lou whirled, but the hallways were filled with black-uniformed patrolmen, stunners in hand. She turned back to the bedroom, ready to break past Josephus and dive through a window.

The administrator raised his hand, and she saw the wand of a stunner. "You must be tired. Sleep now, and we'll talk in the morning." She felt a momentary sting, then nothing else.

Mary Elouise awoke slowly. She stared at the dark, slender man and wondered who he was. The woman beside him also looked familiar. She blinked and realized the woman was her mother. The man was Josephus. She whimpered and tried to roll over, to go back to sleep. Josephus grasped her shoulders and shook her.

"Have some tea, dear," said her mother. They waited while she sat up and drank. After several minutes, her eyes focused and she put down the cup.

"Anita?"

"You're home, dear. Josephus brought you in quite early. It appears you've been bad."

Josephus chuckled. He upended his palm and three metal cubes rolled onto the table. "Memory cubes. You planned to use one on me?"

"It was for Yakov," Mary Elouise said. "I promised."

"Whom?" said Anita.

"My former gardener, an incompetent. I was rather harsh on him." He fingered the cubes. "Stolen memories . . . There was Brosklaw, of course. Who else? We've had several reports."

"There were three more; a woman, two men. They were lucky people with power and accomplishments. They were gifts of birth. I gave their memories to cripples I found wandering out beyond the greenbelt."

Anita pursed her lips. "You've been a very bad girl."

"Me?" Cougar Lou glared. "Don't condescend like that. I'm not a girl any more."

Josephus slapped his palm down hard on the table and laughed. "Who is condescending? Do you think that murder by memory-theft and the gift of those memories to persons you deem less fortunate isn't condescending?"

"No."

"Child, you've got a lot to learn."

"What are you going to do?"

Anita said, "You must be disciplined."

"Punished," said Josephus. "It's an ugly word, but it's more what I had in mind."

"The steel rod?"

"Nothing so brutal. You must realize that memory retrieval holds a good deal more than the historical romances you absorbed for so long. You'll experience some of the less pleasant memories. My special selection."

"You disgust me," said Cougar Lou.

Josephus grinned again. "I think about a thousand subjective years will be appropriate. Then you'll get your old body back."

"I'd already decided that."

"What do you mean?"

Cougar Lou smiled; then the smile slowly diminished. "You were waiting. How did you know?"

"How do you think?"

They took her out then, and in the hall her three husbands were waiting.

"Which one of you sons of bitches was it?" Cougar Lou demanded. "Who betrayed me?" She glared at Nels. "You? You got me the cubes from the institute."

"It could be any one of us," said Macy. "Or all. You talk in your sleep."

"Was it you?"

"Who's to know which you would have rejected?" Macy

spread his hands noncommittally. "It doesn't matter. Who loved you more? To whom would betrayal matter the most?"

"It matters the most to me."

"From what book did you steal that?" said Macy.

She stared at him until he looked away. "No book," said Cougar Lou. "My life." Josephus reached for her elbow, to lead her out; she jerked free.

FREE CITY BLUES

by Gordon Eklund

In the three or four years since Gordon Eklund be-gan writing science fiction he's published an impressive number of excellent stories, ranging from his very first, the well-remembered novelette "Dear Aunt Annie," through novels like Beyond the Resurrection. *The reasons go beyond mere style or craft: Eklund's stories are enlivened by the talents of a real storyteller who likes the people he writes about. See, for instance, this not entirely picaresque novelette about a girl with psi powers in the San Francisco dome-city of tomorrow (a story which incidentally comes complete with an auctorial bow in the direction of Charles Dickens).*

WHEN THE dome clock struck twelve noon, sending shivers of sound reverberating brightly through the green square of the park below, the two ladies—equally middle-aged and first-degree—turned to each other, smiling benignly, and bowed from the waist. One of the two was rather tall, though not quite seven feet, and exceedingly thin, while the second was nearly as round as the other was long. Together, they stood poised upon the top step of the concrete stairs that led from the green park below to the flat gray deck of the observation platform above. The platform itself was already fulsomely occupied by a massive moving statue of a forty-niner miner, who panned for mineral wealth in the narrow blue river which swept majestically across the platform, disappearing inside the concrete at both ends.

After the ringing of the clock, the ladies turned back, gazing once more at the milling crowd which filled the park below. The thin lady moved her eyes carefully, shifting her gaze quickly, like the motions of a hawk circling an unsuspecting chicken flock. The fat lady did not seem to be able to make herself stand still. She kept moving from flat bare foot to flat bare foot in a rhythmic graceless shuffle step.

Then the thin one saw something. Her arm jerked like an arrow shot from a crossbow and she cried, "Oh my Lord! Look! Don't miss this! Have you ever seen such a sight?" Her finger pointed at a solitary figure amid the crowd below.

"Oh my," the round lady said, frowning. "No—no. I swear that's a real sack she's wearing."

"It is." The thin lady waved her pointing finger furiously. "And her *hair*. My God, I have to swear. I say you could raise chickens in that . . . that thatch."

"No," said the other, with a heavy, limping smile. "You're wrong. Not chickens—no—but eagles. You could raise eagles in there."

Hearing this, the thin lady became serious. "I imagine it won't be long until the lesser elements find her. I frankly think it is a real pity. The poor girl. Can you imagine . . . ? Well, I do wish . . . They prey on her sort."

"They have no real choice in the matter," the round lady answered crisply. (And frankly.) "These girls come here looking for it. They seek humiliation. Openly. I've seen it often enough. Working down there among them. Trying to help. I ought to know."

"They are a stupid lot," the thin lady admitted.

"But—of course!"

"And also—oh my God! Look! I swear she's coming this way. Do you think she could have heard?"

"No. Hush. Yes. Don't pay her the slightest attention." Whisperings: "She ought to know better."

Silence ensued as a lone figure emerged from the milling crowd and ascended the stairs. The girl paused on the step just below the two ladies. Her dress was a loose floppy sack, her feet were bare and black, and her hair would have made a fine nesting place for hens. The girl surveyed the two ladies with contempt.

Then, as quickly as she had come, she faded back into the crowd.

"Well!" said the round lady. "Have you—?" Then she laughed shrilly. "My God, the nerve of that . . . that . . ."

"The police will hear of this. I can assure you I will go—" And then this lady—it was the thin lady—stopped talking. Instead, she began to squawk and cackle. Her hands slid neatly into her armpits, as though accustomed to residing there, and her elbows began to flutter. On dainty tiptoes, she pranced down the steps, leaping from one to another, squawking all the while, cackling passionately, arms fluttering like the wings of a landlocked bird. With a graceful swoop, her nose glided down to the concrete and her tongue flicked out, gathering in bits of refuse and spilled food. She pecked furiously at the steps, cackling as she savored each delicious morsel of garbage, the volume of her cries rising as she proceeded inexorably toward the grass below.

Meanwhile, the round lady, who had at first watched her companion silently, now began to moo. She drew one breast —a hefty elongated structure closely resembling a flattened cannonball—from within her bodice and waved it mournfully at the crowd, as if pleading. "Moo," she cried painfully. "Oh, moo."

Moo?

Squawk?

Cackle?

Two such fine ladies as these—so carefully certain and pure in their first-degree?

So it was.

Some ten yards from the platform, arms and legs firmly latched around the width of a lamppost, the girl in the sack, her hair flaring as a wind emerged, watched the scene, laughing with unrestrained glee. Her teeth glistened fiercely white as she laughed, and so genuine, so wonderful was her joy that Andrew could not help approaching.

He removed her gently from around the post, then held her warmly in his arms, stroking her sack as though it were bare flesh. "Please tell me your name," he begged, whispering.

"Duck," she said.

"Uh. What?" Andrew was a nephew of the round lady. He had accompanied her here today. But it was this sack girl— the one who said her name was Duck—whom he presently loved without end.

"I said it was Duck," said Duck.

"What?" said Andrew.

"Oh, Rodelphia," she said, her patience at an end. Then hastily, before he could once more say "what?" she added, "And you're the duck."

"What?" said the duck.

Rodelphia left him quacking madly in the soft fluttering eternally springtime grass of the park. When she was sufficiently far away, her conscience began to ache, so, taking pity upon him, she sent him forward and allowed him to join his aunt and her friend upon the steps. That way all three of them were together, and this was enough to satisfy Rodelphia's sense of rightness.

That day, upon the steps leading to the observation platform, for a full quarter of an hour before the arrival of the police, Union Square Park was graced by the following: (1) a mooing, pleading cow with an exposed udder; (2) a squawking, cackling chicken who ate garbage; and (3) a madly quacking young duck. It was the duck who caused the greatest difficulty when he insisted upon trying to float in the artificial river that flowed past the statue of the forty-niner. Unfortunately, when the duck tried this, he sank with the dull suddenness of a two-hundred-pound man, a creature he happened to closely resemble.

What the whole thing was—it was decided—was a scandal.

When the Free City Chief of Police, Kendrick Drake, was at last allowed to interrogate the trio of surrogate animals, their squawking and quacking and mooing having for the moment ceased, he could not discover a single really solid fact. "I remember nothing—and if I could, I certainly would not choose to discuss it." "My mind is a total blank except—no, I simply cannot remember." When informed that the chief's name was Drake, the man named Andrew immediately became hostile and had to be restrained physically. The two ladies were eventually allowed to return to their ocean-front homes while the young man was held for the night in the county jail. An intoxicant test was administered, but the results proved negative.

Rodelphia, who was blocks away from the park before the police arrived, was shocked by the contrasting conditions prevalent here in the Free City. The tall, stately towers near the floater terminal quickly gave way to smaller two- and three-story houses, the rotting wood and flaking plaster of which seemed to exude the powerfully musty odor of decay. Then she realized there was human excrement here and there in the gutters. She paused to examine this phenomenon but could make nothing of it. Children flocked everywhere, flowing past her in small, strutting, prancing groups. Her mind was jambled with untranslatable phrases: *Gotegetadaw* and *Sumdayagunbebigga* and *Whazamatwityaaenwa*, the thoughts of these passing children; and Rodelphia soon had to admit that she would have to close down her mind entirely before they succeeded in driving her screwy. She did so, remembering how Grandfather had warned her, mincing not a word, "In the Free City there's just three kinds of people, all different. One is the first-degree kind, who is both rich and smart. The second-degree kind is nothing. They do all the work and are famous for being bland, like that meat I got two weeks ago which wasn't real. Remember that? And the third-degree: well, they talk a whole different language. They ain't hardly people."

Nor were they.

Rodelphia's grandfather had resided here in the Free City at one time, back before he had come and stolen her away from the Home, but he would never say what degree he had been, if any. "Couldn't stand the constant noise," he explained, though for her the noise itself was grand—she only regretted she could not comprehend its meaning. The eyes of these children appeared dead, their mouths hung flaccid with decay, and their skin was either incredibly pale or else black as a starless night. Without the noise that came from their minds, she might easily have mistaken them for a lot of marvelously animated walking corpses. Opening her mind once more briefly, she caught a passing thought, *Girlwudya?* and shut things off again, pleased by this comforting reminder of the continuing jamble of daily life about her. God, she was falling in love with this city. Its immemorial jambling and hooting. Above, in bright sparkling scarlet letters as tall as the tallest downtown buildings, the dome cried out: TWO OCLOCK EXACTLY FCT WHILE DISTURBANCE TODAY UNION SQ WHEN 3 1-D CITIZENS PERFORMED BIZARRE ACTS WHILE MIXED CROWD WATCHED UNDER FULL POLICE INVESTIGA- TION PRESENT MOMENT OF POSSIBLE EXTERIOR SUBVERSIVE INFLUENCES COMPLETE REPORT TO FOLLOW K DRAKE CH OF POLICE. Rodelphia stopped cold, her head tilting, eyes pointed at the artificially painted sky. Reading, she laughed. Grandfather had also warned her never to reveal her powers openly. "It's the true reason why I had to flee the home of my fathers and the Free City in turn. They came yipping at my heels and my best frock coat got caught in the Golden Gate as I slipped toward the redwoods that night. Had they caught me, they darn well would have burned me, and I don't mean my frail old body, I mean my mind, which is still as keen and sharp as a slickman's polished blade." She knew he was right, admitted the fact openly to herself, always had, but those two old ladies with their cackling—they had both been so brazen and vulnerable, an irresistible combination. The young man too.

Even as a child, Rodelphia had been unable to withstand open temptation. In the third grade, there was a time when she had made the teacher—an apprentice spinster in her late twenties—expose her naked underbriefs before the gathered class, front and back, then remove them in a brisk singular motion—with pink roses imprinted upon the azure silk— holding them high like a fluttering dove and then proceeding to lecture the class upon the divine nature of such objects, meanwhile rubbing the garment passionately up against her own bare pink cheeks.

Rodelphia had been an incredible sophisticate for that place and time, with any man's mind wide open for her to see, and she had rocked with laughter, watching the humbling of her enemy, but that same night she and Grandfather had moved again, crawling higher up the white slopes of the cold Sierras, plunging ever deeper into the lonely mysteries of the deep backwoods. After turning twelve, she had never seen another human being in the flesh except for Grandfather until yesterday when she caught the floater. When she was fourteen, seeing the turn of the old man's thoughts, she had allowed him to seduce her one warm red night when the whole of the sky was ablaze with a thundering fire. Afterward, bawling painfully upon her bared chest, he pleaded to be forgiven, admitting that he wasn't really her grandfather and couldn't very well be expected to help himself.

"Go ahead and tell me," she said, knowing it had to come.

His tale poured out of him: "Hell, I was only thirty-three when I got away and couldn't have been your grandfather even if I'd've wanted to. I'm not a bit of your blood, my darling. I wish I was closer to you, but when I left the Free City with them yipping 'Mutie, mutie, mutie!' at my heels and came sneaking along various cold back roads, I passed this huge white house with gables and turrets and a million lights, green willowy grass out front and trees in the yard like a miniature forest. I thought it could have been a real country mansion and I stopped, almost thinking I saw a cow grazing in the yard, freezing through and through, hungry enough to gnaw at my own hand, and I started listening to see if I might find a receptive welcome. Instead, near knocked this old head off of its supporting shoulders, on account of what I got was kids—these thousands of kids—all blaring back at me in a horrible cacophony and I started to shut off in a dreadful fright when suddenly I realized there was something more to this than simple noise alone. I listened again, as keenly as I knew how; near panicked realizing that it wasn't only me listening, but there was another in that house who was listening right back at me. I tell you, I shivered, and it wasn't only for the cold night. And it was you, my dumpling granddaughter. You, who was then eight years old and pretty as a roving butterfly, locked up in that awful home of a prison, declaimed as an orphan of the state. You had the power, and it was so darn strong I couldn't believe it, stealing around the house that night, moving on the tips of my toes as I watched out for them phony watchdogs, not seeing a one, grabbing you out of that bed, and running with you, just running. I think we were lucky to get away. And I decided, sleeping that night in a ditch, with you laying on top of me so as not to get damp, that I'd tell you how I was your grandfather and we both had the power on account of our blood. But it was never so, my darling. I don't know why you've got it or even why I've got it. But we do."

And he continued sobbing, and she held him warmly, their relationship at last upon an equal and mature footing, and she stifled a laugh. Not because she was cruel: the laugh was because everything he had just told her, the words pouring out of him like fire from a dragon's mouth, she had plucked piecemeal from his mind years before, knowing the whole story long before she turned ten. Grandfather's powers had always been minimal compared to hers, and he never heard a thought of hers she did not intend for him to hear. But she loved him. Later that night he admitted he had only come to the Free City as a refugee and had lived there less than four years before his exposure. He had, in fact, been born someplace called Nebraska. But she knew this, too, and could never understand why it shamed him so.

After that one occasion, he never touched her body again, but when the old man died, Rodelphia gently tore his body apart molecule by molecule and took the component parts lovingly in the grasp of her mind and then heaved them spinning, high, high , tossing them straight toward the blazing disk of the noontime sun. It was a grand funeral. She loved him that much. After spending one more night inside the cabin, she blew it down the following morning and then hopped down the mountain to the nearest floater station. From there, the Free City was less than two hours away.

Now her tail end was getting sore from sitting. She began to thirst for action. She was tired of walking and also hungry. This place drove her screwy, the way they kept switching the weather every five minutes. Right now a brisk wind was madly blowing. The children, gathered around her in a loose circle, shouted what she guessed were obscenities, but not a word made any real sense to her.

But then, abruptly, a hand snaked around her mouth and another enclosed her jaw. She was lifted right off the curb and dragged, the heels of her feet scratching the concrete, across the sidewalk. The mind behind was thinking, *Hold her, hold her,* so she let him hold her. The children stared after her and one small cute boy laughed aloud, but the girl beside him turned and slapped his face so fiercely that his lower lip split, exposing blood. A dark doorway opened behind her and she was drawn through it, swallowed by a dimness that was not quite blackness.

The boy set her down in the dust, then scurried around with a finger upon his slender lips. "I won't hurt you," he whispered.

"I know," she said.

She was crouched inside the basement of one of the ramshackle houses. A rat came scurrying up—a ghostly gray specter—and sniffed at her feet, then bounded hastily back as she gave its brain a tickle. The boy sauntered back, returning from having shut the door. The dimness was now much nearer to real darkness, but behind, deep in the bowels of the basement, she could hear the sound of other voices.

The boy said, "He told me to bring you. That was the only way I know how. I'm sorry, but if I'd missed, if you'd got away . . ." He drew his forefinger swiftly across his throat and then gurgled passionately on his own imagined blood.

"Who's he?" asked Rodelphia.

"Why, Abraham."

"Oh, sure," she said. "Him."

"You've never heard of Abraham?"

"In the Bible." She pretended to ponder. "And Lincoln." The subject bored her. "Tell me your name"—though she knew.

"I'm Hungry," he said.

"Oh, really?" she said. "So am I," laughing.

But he had plainly heard this one before. "I can't imagine your never having heard of Abraham. Are you sure you're not lying? If you don't know him, how come you're down here? You're not a third, and you're nothing else, so you've got to be a derelict."

"I hopped off the floater three hours ago."

"From where?"

She waved toward the east. Where she thought the east must lie.

"And they let you in?" He pointed at her sack dress while his eyes made puzzled circles in her hair. "You?"

"I snuck in," she confessed.

"I thought so but—" A fierce bellow cut him short. The sound came rumbling like thunder through the hollow twisting corridors of the basement, dashing like the heaving waters of a flash flood streaming down a dry Western riverbed. *"Where are you, Hungry?"* came the bellow.

The boy leaped to his feet and shouted back in a shrill, piping voice, "Right here, Abraham!"

"You got that girl?" came the rumble.

"Yes sir!"

"Then bring her here! Goddamn the Lord! Quit fooling around!"

"Quick," said Hungry, pulling her upright.

Rodelphia shook him away. "Hands off me!" she cried extra loud.

Hungry paled at the sound of her voice, backing away, cowering, hands shielding his face.

"Oh, come on. I'm not going to hit you," Rodelphia said,

leading him away through the twisting mazelike passages of the basement. As they rounded each new corner, a tiny electric light glowed at their appearance. The room they sought was the center room—the prize at the middle of the maze —a tiny, cluttered, cloistered place filled with the stored junk and refuse of the hundred lives that were lived above. A child sat here upon the broken remnants of a couch, another on the floor scrawled her name carelessly in the dust, while a third child—a golden-haired boy—dangled like a cobweb from the rafters above. Maybe two dozen children in all— sliced neatly down the middle according to sex. An average age was probably sixteen. The girls seemed older than the boys.

"Hungry!" bellowed Abraham, seeing them coming. He sat sprawled in the very midst of his children, a giant wobble of a man, big and powerful as a whale, with a fierce jagged black beard dangling clear to his chest and red-painted lips that curled deliberately downward at their ends and blue eyes that managed to twinkle and glower simultaneously. He was dressed wholly in black rags, tattered torn fragments of cloth, a brazen combination of the styles and fashions of a generation. A stovepipe hat tottered precariously upon his head like a crown upon the head of a medieval prince.

He did not move, saying, "I am Abraham," mocking politeness as Rodelphia strolled fearlessly forward. Then he stretched his hand toward hers. "Aha," and he kissed her palm delicately.

"You're lovely," he murmured. Then: "Kids out!" evoking a rustling and bustling so tinged with undue haste that Rodelphia felt it necessary to close down her mind once more.

Then she and Abraham were alone except for Hungry, who lurked inconspicuously beside the doorway. Perhaps he was acting as a guard. But for whom? she wondered, finding his thoughts unclear on this point. Suddenly he tilted forward, so as not to miss a single word.

"Do you know us?" Abraham said. "We are thieves."

She confessed her ignorance, sitting beside him. A recent arrival in the Free City. She explained everything. A displaced citizen from the near east. Innocent, she was. And lonely.

"Poor child. But I could have told you that," Abraham said. "We are simple people, mere thieves only. I hope you do not misunderstand me as—" He licked his lips in obvious preparation for an extended dissertation. His tongue flamed red as the lipstick smeared. "We have a point." Slamming his fist into the ground, raising an emphasizing puff of dust. "More than that. We have a purpose. We steal, yes, but that is hardly all. Now you tell me—believing it as you speak—you say, 'Abraham, stealing is wrong.' You say, 'Stealing is a sin and you are a most evil man.' And what do you expect from me in reply? A spasm of guilt? Anguish? Should I say, 'My child, why yes, you are absolutely correct?' And kiss you boldly upon the lips, repenting, and thus surrendering my profession, my livelihood. My life, in fact. Ho-ha! Stealing is not wrong! I'm telling you that it carries both point and purpose. In this society we have three worlds. The first which is idle and rich, the second which works to feed the others, and the third which is nothing. All right—but what of the others? The humble few? I mean us." Thumping his chest. "Or just me, my love. We who are called derelicts, rejected by all, rejecting in turn. My story? I was born a first as most of my children were born seconds. I lived a most contented life. My mother was a lovely wisp of a woman, rumored to be close to a hundred in years, an original survivor of the first moon colony, and a lady never known to speak in a voice harsher than a whisper. My father was a lisping pervert, a lover of boys—a walking archetype of that form, or perhaps merely a cliché, a stereotype—with a wrist bent a full ninety degrees, creating me purely by mistake, wandering into the wrong bed one deluded night, mistaking my mother's graceful rump for that of some boy, implanting the seed which grew to be me by slip alone. That is my family story, as told by servants, aunts, uncles—it's something I heard my whole life. My father had gone to America in shame—New York, I think—and my mother died of cancer. At the side of her warm grave, these eyes"—pointing at the simultaneously twinkling/glowering orbs, already close to overflowing with moistness—"shed bitter tears, true tears of anguish and despair, wet and filled with the angry cruel salt of honest grief, and never since—not for one second—have I cried. I came here, living first in the sewers below, devoted to pits of the purest foul hell, then crawling on my belly this high to a damp, cold basement. True, we steal—myself and my children. We take from those who have it to spare and bestow these blessings upon those less fortunate—namely, ourselves. Or me." He wept openly now, shedding unashamed rivers of tears. "We have no intention, however, of harming the fabric of this society. We care not to bring it down upon our own ears. Anarchism is a monstrous aberration. We spit upon those who profess it." He spat in the dust. "We love and adore this free city. And we do our part; yes, we steal.

"So will you join us?" And he began to cough, the noise rising so high it clouded his mind and prevented Rodelphia from peering within. She waited until he was through.

"Cancer of the lungs," he explained. "As my poor mother died."

"Isn't there something you can do about it?" she asked, genuinely concerned.

"I could swallow pills." He popped a pill into his mouth. "But I refuse."

"You do?"

"I prefer a natural death to an unnatural life." A gentle cough—a prompt answering pill. "But will you not join us?"

She said, "All right."

"And you will steal?"

"I will."

"Then remove your clothes. That foul sack. Ugh."

"My clothes?"

"Yes. Ugh. I'm afraid that it's necessary. Absolutely. Please don't mind me. I see that your upbringing has emphasized the proper virtues. As did mine. Because of my mother, I have remained a virgin to this day. Tell her, Hungry."

"Abraham is a virgin," said Hungry, from the doorway.

"So tell her why."

"Abraham is waiting for a woman he can love."

"And he has not yet found her," Abraham said, sniffling. "See? I prefer unnatural abstinence to natural lust."

"And you don't take pills either?" she asked.

"Either strip or die," he said coldly.

She guessed he meant it. His mind was a horrible mess. Working the dress over her head was the work of a moment. Beneath, she was naked. Hungry disappeared during the act of undressing, but promptly returned carting a full-length mirror, cracked in a dozen places, lines radiating from the various epicenters of destruction like the slender strands of a spider's web. Hungry held the mirror so that Abraham could see the girl in its reflection. Abraham, staring at the glass, muttered. Rodelphia, glancing down, saw nothing exceptional. She did regret not having washed more recently.

Spinning on her tiptoes, flapping her arms, she gave her hips an abruptly furious rattle. She felt silly doing this, but it was what he wanted.

"Splendid," said Abraham, finally. Looking away, he drew his beard over his lips, rubbed, then let it flop back to his chest. He wasn't looking at Rodelphia any more.

She got dressed.

"Retain the sack," he said. "It hides your charms and will force them to wonder."

"Who will wonder?"

He explained her work: she was to be a prostitute, performing the proper functions for a proper fee. "But make certain you capture their money banks before letting them get away. I mean, don't let them keep a penny. If they have nothing, call Hungry, who will administer a beating. This rarely happens. Hungry will provide further information. I believe you're worth it—whether you know it or not."

A cry erupted from the outer corridor, and then the door crashed open and a small slender girl came bounding inside, her white hair flying behind. "Father—I cut myself," she cried, rushing to plop herself in Abraham's wide lap.

"Poor girl," he said, looking down, parting the trickle of blood upon the child's knee, exposing a small jagged gash.

"On a nail," she said.

He stroked her hair, drawing the girl lovingly close to his chest. He rocked back and forth, shifting on his hips. "Won't you be all right?" he asked.

"Oh, yes," she said, smiling now.

"I will care for you. I will."

"I know," she said.

Rodelphia turned and tiptoed from the room. Hungry followed her. He shut the door. Through the wood, they heard the child give an awful shriek.

"I think he hit her," Rodelphia said.

Hungry, looking embarrassed, shrugged. He led her away.

"That's his daughter?" she asked.

He said, "Sure."

"And the mother?"

He shrugged again.

Later, as they stood on the street, he explained. "Abraham loves us, all of us, and that means you. But don't cross him. He'll kill you if you try. What he wants from us is money, not love. He gives all the love that's needed around here."

Then he left her standing in the middle of the gutter. She was careful to avoid the pockets of excrement but followed the rest of his instructions explicitly. She held her hands clasped in front of her waist, let her shoulders slump like those of a hunchback and allowed her tongue to dangle freely from the left corner of her mouth. Past this obstruction, she murmured ambiguous noises in a light, lilting voice. She guessed he knew what he was up to.

Then it got dark all of a sudden. The sun fell straight down out of the sky and was replaced a moment later by a full yellow moon and a blanket of brilliant stars. Around her, street lamps blossomed into full illumination and puzzling sounds began to echo along the block—she could have sworn she heard crickets. Then a man approached from the shadows across the way. He came stomping straight toward her, wearing a pair of thigh-length leather boots and a green suede belt wrapped so tightly around his waist that his belly flopped above and over it, though the man was hardly fat.

"I . . . er . . . you know," he said, removing his money bank from under his arm. Unzipping the purse, he jiggled the coins. He said, "You poor thing," and took her hand in his.

She continued to sing, but he appeared ready to go. She gave him a brief wave, then turned and twitched herself as if stung by a hornet and skipped off into the basement behind. She heard him following.

In the first room, a light had been fired for her benefit. It clearly showed the rumpled legless bed in the farthest corner. "We won't need that," said the man. Purely for fun, Rodelphia said, *"Imwannapleememan,"* which was third-degree talk. She had been warned not to try it. "Nobody can talk the way they can. They've been bred for it since two hundred years ago. Don't try." But she had never been one for following instructions.

The man did not object. In fact, the sound of her voice, grunting through the thicket of the words, had clearly thrilled him. Now he sat on the bed and begged her to sit beside him. Before doing so, she crept gently into his mind and saw what he wanted her to do. It almost made her laugh.

She sat beside him while he flounced her hair and tickled her leg.

"Some are born more fortunate than others," the man said. "That is the way of the world. But don't you agree with me that it is the duty of the fortunate to aid those less fortunate?"

She nodded, wide-eyed.

"See?" He clapped his hands. "That is very good." He was pleased at her quickness. "And that is why I have come here tonight. At home, I possess a full complement of children. The boy is so painfully bright that I weep when I hear him. I am convinced he will amount to something royal. My daughter is too young for brains yet, though I have detected a creative bent in the manner of her walk. My wife does social work. I wouldn't be surprised if you had met her. Myself, you ask: my position is an essential one. You have been to Broadway? No, of course you haven't. Poor child, you cannot. But I am the one who composes the jokes, the riddles and witty sayings, that are inscribed each night upon the dome out there for the benefit of the celebrants. Every evening, I prowl Broadway and listen to the eruptions of spontaneous laughter that greet my work. For instance, *How is an android like an American?* I did that. My work. And others. I'm very good at it. Shall we get ready?"

Standing, Rodelphia removed her dress. The man looked her up and down, smiled, and then darted a glance toward the corner where the mud buckets waited. He then removed his boots and belt. Rodelphia gave a sigh. Enough was quite enough. She started the pictures going for him, then hopped away. She would do almost anything for the experience, but she wasn't going to roll around in mud. Besides, she was starved, sapped of all energy. Why didn't they feed her around here? On the bed, the man groaned and panted, his breath coming like the wind off the sea.

Before he finished, she stepped forward and lifted his money bank. She set the coins in the corner beside the mud buckets. Then she let her conjured image merge with her physical presence.

The man was frowning at her, puzzled by his cleanliness and hers. She gave a shrug, letting him wonder, and began to dress. In a quick voice, he told her, "It's only fair this way. I know you can't understand why. You probably don't care. But we've rubbed mud over you people for two hundred years. We've kept you the way you are, never given you a chance. But I'm not guilty. How can I be? I know what has to be done to keep society on an even footing. I'm no anarchist. I believe in rule and reason." He checked his money bank, but finding it empty, merely shrugged. "All fine," he muttered. She followed him to the door. Without looking, he patted her back. "I do hope I'll see you again. I'll try to have a few of my jokes translated. Then we can laugh together. More fun that way. I suppose the riddles would prove too esoteric for you. A pity. My best work is my riddles. I've got a fine one tonight: What did the deer say when the archer's arrow missed him by a fraction of an inch? But you wouldn't know. Be seeing you." The night swallowed him.

Rodelphia dressed, then returned to the gutter. Hungry, who had been hiding across the street, raced over. "How did it go?" Before answering, she demanded food. He said no, that was impossible. "Think of someone else for a change. Abraham would kill me if I let you go now."

He wanted to know how it had gone.

"Just great," she said.

"He was first-degree. Was it the mud?"

"Yes."

"That's best. Sometimes we get a second-degree. The firsts feel sorry for the thirds, but the seconds just hate them. It can get nasty."

"How?" she asked.

She found out several moments later, when a band of second-degree toughs dashed from a dark doorway, shoved

Hungry flat on his face, and carried her away into the basement. She was in there with them for more than an hour.

When the boys came out, emerging one by one, the last wiping his slickman's knife upon his shirttail, Hungry raced across to see if she was still alive.

She was. At her side sat a huge stack of glinting coins.

"Now can I eat?" she asked.

He had to tell her no.

Back to the gutter again. From there to the basement. As the early evening wandered into middle night, Rodelphia served an additional six clients. By the time the last departed, her patience had reached its end. She streaked across the street with the rapidity of a greyhound racer and pulled Hungry loose from the shadows.

"I quit," she said.

"How much money have you made?"

She told him plenty and took him in and made him look at the neatly stacked coins. He gave a whistle. "Come on— let's tell Abraham."

Abraham was alone in the center room. He was fast asleep. His snores ripped through the still air like the growling of a great angry beast. From the doorway Hungry pelted his boss with small flat stones. He had picked them up on the street.

When Abraham awoke, Hungry and Rodelphia entered the room.

Rubbing his eyes, Abraham said, "How goes it?"

Rodelphia deposited the coins in front of him. They fell to the floor in a clattering mess.

Abraham uttered a gleeful cry. "This is wonderful. Darling, I said you could do it. Now I know that I love you."

"But she didn't do it," Hungry said.

Rodelphia groaned. She looked into his mind and saw what his game was. But it was too late to try to stop him.

"How about something to eat?" she said, hoping to forestall the coming crisis.

But it didn't work. Abraham sprang to his feet and raced across the room. Catching Hungry by the collar, he said, "What do you mean by that?"

"She's a mutie," said Hungry.

"So what?" He let Hungry go. "Do I care?"

She might not have been there for all the attention they were paying her. She prowled the room in search of food, finding a stale prune on the floor near the back wall. But it left a mean nasty lump in her stomach.

"She must have been playing pictures for them," Hungry said. "I watched the way you told me, and she had seven or eight first-degree customers and there wasn't a drop of mud used out of the buckets. Explain that. And a gang of seconds jumped her. Must have been twelve in the pack. They had her for an hour. And she's still alive. Have her strip. I bet you won't find even a bruise."

Abraham turned upon her, clearly considering Hungry's suggestion. "I have nothing against muties," he said.

"Good," said Rodelphia. "But I'm not taking off my clothes again no way."

A knife appeared in Abraham's huge hand. She could have sworn he'd got it from his beard. He dashed at her, swinging the knife. She made her molecules jump and landed on the opposite side of the room.

"Careful doing that," Hungry said. He edged toward the door. "I don't want you landing on me." Then he ran.

Abraham came at her again. She took another jump. Grandfather had warned her never to try this trick in public. It was probably just as well that he was dead now and couldn't see her.

When she was whole again, she asked Abraham to stop. "You'll never catch me," she said.

He didn't need to be told. Already he was panting furiously from exertion. He sat down on the floor and began to weep. "I'm sorry, but I just can't allow my customers to be cheated.

I have a reputation to maintain. And self-pride. As a matter of fact, I happen to love and admire muties. Like myself, they are rebels. But I'm afraid you'll just have to go, my little darling." He threw his knife suddenly but his aim was poor and his thrust was weak and the blade caught in the hem of her dress. By the time she managed to extract the knife, he was coming at her again.

This time, closing her eyes, she pictured a brilliant image of the outside gutter. She jumped.

And landed whole.

But Hungry stood at her side only inches away.

"That was close," he said.

"Why did you tell him?" She sat on the curb. "You know, you don't make much sense."

He admitted as much, sitting up close to her. "I love you," he said.

"I know. That's what puzzles me. You're not supposed to act that way when you love somebody."

"Why not? I knew he'd never hurt you. I just couldn't see you wasting your life working for him. At least not tonight. I wanted to take you sightseeing with me. I couldn't think of any other way of getting you away from him. And he hates muties. I like them myself. At least"—he laid his hand lovingly upon hers—"I don't have anything against you."

"Can we eat now?" she asked.

He opened his fist proudly, displaying a glittering roll of gleaming coins. "We eat like a Mayor Dempsey."

She laughed in spite of herself. "Is that good?"

"The best. But first you've got to come with me."

"Where?" she asked, standing.

"This way." He led her down the avenue to the corner, where a narrow steel-and-glass rectangular booth sat bathing in its own brilliant light. Above the booth a neon sign flickered, proclaiming: TRANSPORT STATION—PUBLIC.

"To Broadway," Hungry said. "North Beach. It's the best

place in the Free City for both eating and seeing. Tomorrow morning I guess we'll come back here. I won't tell on you tomorrow, if we get everything done tonight, so you can go ahead and work for him if you still want."

"I don't think he'll want me. You took care of that."

"Oh, no." He fell into a secretive whispering tone that tickled her ear. "You don't have to worry about that. Abraham uses drugs. He swallows them like a big fish after minnows. His favorite is *Blank*—that's a drug where you take it and it erases your memory like a big brush. Among other things. Every night Abraham takes a huge dose of *Blank*. In the morning he wakes up and the only thing he knows is his own name. He's got that tattooed on his wrist. Everything else, I have to come in and tell him. What he is and why he is and what all he's up to."

"But that can't be true," she said. Hungry opened the glass door of the booth and went inside. She waited, watching him play with various dials and buttons upon the farthest wall. She saw a street map of the Free City and a beeping red dot that roamed through the streets as Hungry manipulated the dials. "He told me so much about his life," Rodelphia said. "Even his childhood. And I could tell it was true."

"Sure," said Hungry. "He thinks it's true. Why not? But I'm the one who makes it all up. That story he told you—about his mother—that's my basic story. But I've got plenty more. I used to really let my imagination run wild but I've had to curb that tendency lately. A couple of weeks ago, I told Abraham he was the legitimate eldest son of the old Chief of Police. You should have seen him. He stalked straight down to City Hall and demanded his job and uniform. It got embarrassing. They locked him up as screwy, and it took days to get him set free."

"But isn't he? Screwy, I mean?"

Hungry came out to explain to her about the booth. It was a public device to be used for getting from one place to another. No fee. Within the limits of the city and county, meaning the dome. He had already set the coordinates for where they wanted to go, so when he was gone, she was to open the door, then close it tightly behind. "And make sure it's closed or it won't work. Then hit the big red button and you'll come right after me."

She said, "Sure."

Jumping through the transport booth was no different from jumping through her own powers except that she didn't know where she was going. But she got there in any event. At the end of the line was another booth identical to the one from which she had jumped. Stepping out, she wasn't even positive she had gone anywhere. Looking around, she was instantly assaulted by the most gorgeous colors. It took a moment for her to realize she was seeing the sky. It had to be the dome, she knew, painted in bursts of swirling red and orange and violet and green and every imaginable shade in between—all constantly shifting, weaving into one another, flowing like water, mingling fantastically, then bursting apart, shattering. Then she noticed there were pictures up there too—faces—for here an eye blinked between clouds of blue and gold, and here in another place was a big round red nose, and then suddenly an Indian chief came riding across a blank portion of the sky mounted upon the back of a huge palomino stallion. The chief threw back his arm and cocked his elbow and then heaved a brilliantly feathered lance straight across the middle of the sky. For a moment the lance burned savagely, and then it plunged into the middle of a churning mass of color and was gone. When Rodelphia looked back, the chief too had disappeared.

"That's not so much," said Hungry, taking her arm.

"Now look at that," he told her.

The dome had gone mysteriously dark. Rodelphia held her breath, anticipating. Then a series of block letters, bright yellow in color, began to appear, one blinking into existence, then another. Softly to herself, she read:

WHAT DID THE DEER SAY WHEN
THE ARCHER'S ARROW
MISSED HIM BY HALF AN INCH?

Not amused, Hungry said, "That was an arrow escape. You know," he said, "I wish the guy that writes that stuff would think up something new for a change."

For the first time—so totally involved had she been with the formations on the dome—Rodelphia took a look at the street. It was literally jammed with people. It was impossible to tell where the street ended and the sidewalk began. Grabbing Hungry's hand tightly, she allowed him to draw her deeply into the middle of the mob. So many separate bristling thoughts hammered at her mind that she had to close it down entirely. Walking within the mob, she saw that the whole was actually only the sum of many component parts. A dozen men and women streamed past, holding hands, whipping in a snakelike dance. Moments later, the snake himself appeared: a huge fat python ridden by a naked yellow-haired girl who was only slightly longer than the snake was wide. Some people simply stood aside and watched the various processions. Among the performers was a bald-headed juggler who, while balancing a stick on the tip of his nose, tossed and caught six bottles, a tin cup, and one live puppy. A toothless, shriveled man crawled up to Rodelphia and asked if she might want to purchase the services of a mutie.

"He's a good one. Four legs on him. Various other deviations from the norm. And he can read your mind like a book."

Hungry gave her a warning look and she politely refused the offer.

Continuing on, they seemed to be moving against the general flow of traffic. Not once did they see the same person twice. Above, the colors had returned to the dome, and tilting back her head Rodelphia watched transfixed while Hungry gave her a rundown on the street. He first warned her to be especially careful, apparently referring back to the toothless man, because these people here were first and they hated muties. "I saw one burned to death—he was hardly a baby—a month ago. And that was nothing. There's been much worse. I can tell you." She promised to be good. The rest of what he said she hardly heard; the colors were so gorgeous. He said, "This street is the true heart of the Free City. Nobody actually lives here, but every night when the sun is closed down this whole street comes alive. I really don't know where some of them come from, but I've heard that many sleep down in the sewers and come up only at night. That way they never have to see the sun, which they hate. I guess you could call it a big party, with the Free City itself serving as host. The party runs nightly from sunset to sunup, and anything can happen and usually does. Come dawn, everybody runs home or down to the sewers or wherever. I thought you'd like it."

She did like it well enough. The whole thing—especially with her mind closed down so that she couldn't really see— was something absolutely beyond her powers to comprehend. It was those things she could not understand that she always liked the best. There really weren't that many.

"In here," said Hungry.

He jumped through a doorway and she went right after him. After the noise of the street, the silence here was dreadful. Rodelphia opened her mind tentatively and catching a thought from Hungry felt much better. A whiff of cooking food caught her nose and she laughed gleefully. At last they would eat. Turning to Hungry, she allowed him to glimpse a smile of complete gratitude.

Then someone caught her hand and gave it a tug. Turning, she saw a happy, smiling man of about thirty-five. With a start she realized he was amazingly handsome: hard as she looked, she couldn't find a flaw; his features were as perfect as chiseled marble. Except for a narrow band around his waist and a leather pouch attached there, he was quite naked.

"My name is Epson," he said. "I wanted to ask if you'd care to accompany me home."

Hungry tried to pull her away, but she stood her ground firmly. Taking a peep into Epson's mind, she discovered that he was someone rich and famous and powerful. This made her pause. Grandfather had suggested she seek out the rich and famous and powerful, for only they could protect her. She had violated so many of his dictums today; wasn't it about time she said yes for a change?

But there was something she had to find out first. "Do you have food at your home?" she asked. "I'm really starved."

"At my home," said Epson, "the food is natural and constantly in readiness."

"Then let's go," she said, taking his hand. Hungry, who was weeping openly now and protesting his love, tried to stop her. She got past him, but then he fell to his knees and clawed at her dress. Another man, going for food, stopped long enough to boot Hungry in the rear. He fell over, hitting his face. When he got himself up again, Rodelphia saw that his nose had turned red and shiny as a beet. She was glad he wasn't badly hurt.

Epson took her back to the street, then darted around an abrupt corner. As if by magic, they were alone; the mob had gone. Epson asked her to stop, then put both arms around her waist. He said, "It is my duty to inform you that you are under arrest."

Rodelphia was a quick thinker. Picturing an image of the street in front of Abraham's basement, she prepared to jump.

Only she didn't jump. Nothing happened. Opening her eyes, there was Epson.

Still thinking quickly, she turned to run.

Only he held her firmly and her feet never moved an inch.

Then something hard and cold snapped around her wrist.

Peering into his mind, she ran smack into an impenetrable stone wall.

Epson said, "I'm afraid you'll have to come along with me, Rodelphia."

The interview took place in Epson's office. The room seemed big since the only furniture was a small wooden desk and a tiny chair. Epson sat on the edge of the desk while Rodelphia took possession of the chair. The ceiling and walls were painted a dingy, ugly shade of gray; the carpet was torn and frayed.

The office was located on the first floor of the Free City Police Headquarters. Rodelphia asked Epson if he was a policeman.

"No, not exactly," he said. "We have only two policemen in this entire city. And I'm not one of them."

"Then who are you?"

He favored her with a bright smile which dripped with kindness. "I'm the same as you," he said. "A mutation. A telepath. I read minds, leap through space in violation of ancient rigid laws of physics. We—you and I—brother and sister." He crossed his first two fingers to illustrate the closeness of their relationship.

"Then why did you go and arrest me?"

"If I were given to dramatics—and I'm not—I would say: Rodelphia, I did it to save your life. It happens to be true."

"Nobody can kill me," she said, with deliberate smugness.

"*I* can. Now I want you to listen to what I say. Will you?"

"Sure." Later she prided herself upon the fact that she had listened to every word he said.

He started out by telling her that she had been in the Free City long enough to know that the social stability of the city was based upon a strict system dividing the entire population into three caste groups. "However," he said, "nature has a way of playing havoc with the best-laid plans. Thus—*presto* —you and I. Little jokes from Mother Nature. We are not, I can assure you, at all unique. Estimates"—he dug some papers out of his desk drawer and sprinkled them randomly across the floor—" show that one of every fifty births in this city is a mutation of some kind. Most—those with the eight heads and fourteen arms—die at once, though a few survive and then are killed." He drew a sharp forefinger across his Adam's apple. "An even smaller number—maybe one in a hundred—escape detection entirely. These are almost always mental mutations such as you and I. Three hundred or so years ago, a massive nuclear bomb exploded near here, spraying radiation upon the city like a rainstorm. The city itself survived, but the people haven't been the same since. It's even worse in America, but that doesn't concern us. Thus the mutations, physical and mental, the most highly developed of which are the telepaths."

She started to ask him about her grandfather, but then noticed that his tongue—purple as a grape—was dangling from one corner of his mouth. The gesture startled her and she forgot what she wanted to say. Then the tongue withdrew and he continued.

"As for you, I'm afraid dear nature has granted you a power. An ability. But—and this is the question—what are you supposed to do with it? Bet you don't know. So far today, I have to tell you, you have used your abilities most unwisely. You have, in fact, revealed yourself in a dangerous fashion. You have been frivolous—the most ugly of sins. Mutations are disliked within the general population of the city. It's the old story of fear becoming hatred. Those that are discovered are invariably murdered. They are by definition unhuman, and to kill one is not a crime. A few derelicts, such as those you chanced to meet today, are tolerated. We pity them deeply. But not mutants. A mutant is both a deviation and a danger. So—" He drew his finger across his throat again, but this time the long nail caught in the puckered flesh, making a tiny cut. Rodelphia watched the gentle trickling of blood.

"Let me tell you a story," Epson said. "I promise you a

moral. I guarantee it." He smiled. "Once there was a man—shall we call him Edgar Tuttle?—who was born a mutant. We'll say that this birth occurred shortly after the bomb, when the Free City was still in the process of finding its feet once more. Tuttle was an intelligent man but not, alas, a wise one. He used his powers frivolously. He inserted thoughts into the minds of others. Beautiful women—often the wives of the rich or powerful—fell constantly in love with him. Handed an insult, Tuttle returned it in kind. His favored enemies paraded the streets of the city, quacking like ducks or mooing like cows. He enjoyed telling people their innermost thoughts and desires when these things happened to be personally embarrassing to them. At the first sign of potential danger, Tuttle leaped through time and space. Does this sound familiar?"

"It does," Rodelphia admitted.

"It should. Well, Tuttle died. He was murdered as he slept. The people of the city caught him and nailed him to a tree or shot him full of holes or cut off his head. Not a pleasant story, no." A tear caught in his eye; he coughed daintily to clear his throat of grief. "But I promised you a moral, and here it is: No matter how strong a man may be, he will never be stronger than all other men put together.

"Now for a second story, a thematic sequel to the first. Our protagonist this time carries the name of Norman Daniels. As a matter of form, let's make him a maternal grandfather of mine, several generations removed. Born shortly after the death of Tuttle, but not realizing the scope of his powers till relatively late in life. When he does, fear grips his heart like an iron vest. He races to city hall and there falls on his knees. He begs the authorities for permission for an immediate operation. He wants the offending portion of his brain excised. Above all, Norman Daniels wishes to be normal again. Wisely, his request is refused. Instead, he is offered an opportunity of putting his talents to good use. He is authorized to visit and inspect all the city's hospitals, specifically the maternity wards. Nothing like setting a mutant to catch a mutant. On his first day, Norman detects ten previously undiscovered mutants. A medal is awarded to him. Mayor Dempsey kisses his cheek. The job becomes his work for life. He performs his assigned tasks with pride and pleasure and dignity. The worse conceivable deviant from the social order, Norman Daniels ensures the continued survival of this same order. And he is successful. When he dies—a satisfied and richly honored man—his replacement is one of the children he himself has discovered. A full circle.

"So you see my point, Rodelphia? This city is an island, surrounded on all sides by hostile, turbulent forces. Our survival is based upon order, decency, regularity, and sanity. We mutants must surrender the capricious possibilities of our powers to the greater good of everyone. If this city falls, civilization falls as well. *Kerplop*. Not a pleasant sound, no. But it happens to include us, Rodelphia dear. You and I."

Suddenly he stopped talking and started laughing hysterically. Falling off the edge of the desk, he hit the floor with a *kerplop*. Down there, he continued to giggle, holding his stomach. Then he stopped, jumped to his feet, and dived for her. She darted away, taking refuge in a corner. "So what do you expect me to do? You don't expect me to start going around to hospitals, do you?"

He shook his head, bringing a lace handkerchief from somewhere and making it flutter beneath his nose. "No, no, of course not. As a matter of fact, there are innumerable tasks you may perform. My personal duties consist primarily of crime detection and prevention. I roam the city night and day like a wandering dog, detecting the presence of criminal thoughts in criminal minds before they can be transformed into criminal deeds. Others operate the dome—the artistically inclined among us. You witnessed the North Beach demonstration tonight. I tell you no two people saw exactly the same thing. Wouldn't you like to have a hand—or is it a mind?—in that? Or you may, if you wish, work among the wayward. Do social work in the third-degree wards. Implanting proper attitudes into youthful half-formed minds. The choice," he said, waving his arms expansively, tottering on his feet, "is yours."

"I'll give it a thought," she pledged.

"Divine!" He clapped his hands fiercely. "Now I want you to come home with me." A nasty smile creased his face, and he came toward her on soundless feet. "Come," he said.

"Will you feed me?" she asked, slipping past his initial assault.

"You bet I will," he said, catching her arms. He held tight.

"Then let's go," she said. "And you let me go."

He released her, following cautiously as they left his office. Outside, it was snowing. Rodelphia stopped on the uppermost step of the concrete porch and gazed upward at the graceful spinning flakes that came cascading gently down from the dome above. Already, a full inch of snow blanketed the ground around the station.

In a hurry, Epson started to rush past her. Then suddenly she saw into his mind. A teeming jungle of jangled thoughts rocked her back on her heels, but she had sufficient presence of mind to insert a tentative hook before she was driven out.

She gave the hook a tug. It held. She had him now.

Stopping cold in his tracks, Daniels turned and looked at her. Then his front teeth thrust past his lower lip, and he turned back. Bending his knees, he jumped, clearing the porch in a single expert bound. A second leap carried him deeply into the blanket of snow. He hopped again. *Hop, hop, hop.* Hands on her hips, Rodelphia watched poor Epson hopping away, a quaint, curious rabbit disappearing into the night, leaving behind a tiny whispering pattern of prints in the soft gentle bright flatness of the fallen snow.

"Serves you right," she said aloud, though she wasn't positive that was exactly true. She had a distinct feeling Epson could no more help being screwy than anyone else in this city.

Suddenly overcome by hunger, she clutched her stomach. Thinking about hunger made her remember poor old Hungry, whom she had deserted. Now there was the one person she had met in this city who didn't seem to be totally screwy. She tried to remember the side street where Epson had captured her, hoping she could go there and look for Hungry on Broadway. She made herself a promise that if she found him again, she would wipe away the thoughts of love she had implanted in his mind. She was curious to know how he would feel about her if left to himself. One way or another, she was going to get something to eat. She hadn't forgotten that either.

As she stood on top of the porch, getting her thoughts in order, a man came hurrying past her. As he went by, she caught a sneering thought directed at her sack dress.

She'd had enough of that for one day.

Here we go again, she thought, and before she could think anything else, the man had flopped to his belly and began to crawl down the steps, slithering gracefully on his stomach. Passing her, he stuck out his tongue and rattled his rump, but she stood stock-still, and he did not strike.

With a shrug, then a laugh, Rodelphia jumped. Someday she was just going to have to learn how to control herself.

But not now.

ABOUT THE EDITOR

Terry Carr has been acclaimed as one of the major editors of modern science fiction. He has received five Nebula Award citations from the Science Fiction Writers of America. Born in Oregon and now living in California, he has received Hugo Award nominations both as author and editor in the field.